IT'S A WONDERFUL LIFE™

IT'S A WONDERFUL LIFE™

M. C. Bolin

HarperPaperbacks
A Division of HarperCollins*Publishers*

HarperPaperbacks

A Division of HarperCollins*Publishers*
10 East 53rd Street, New York, N.Y. 10022-5299

This is a work of fiction. The characters, incidents, and dialogues are
products of the author's imagination and are not to be construed as
real. Any resemblance to actual events or persons, living or dead,
is entirely coincidental.

It's a Wonderful Life © 1947 Liberty Films, Inc. Republic Entertainment Inc. and
"It's a Wonderful Life" are trademarks of Republic Entertainment Inc.®,
a subsidiary of Spelling Entertainment Group Inc.®

ISBN: 0-06-101176-2

HarperCollins®, ■®, and HarperPaperbacks™
are trademarks of HarperCollins*Publishers* Inc.

HarperPaperbacks may be purchased for educational, business, or sales promo-
tional use. For information, please write:
Special Markets Department, HarperCollins*Publishers*,
10 East 53rd Street, New York, N.Y. 10022-5299.

Novelization provided by Creative Media Applications.

Printed in the United States of America

First printing: November 1996

Designed by Michele Bonomo

Library of Congress Cataloging-in-Publication Data
is available from the publisher.

Visit HarperPaperbacks on the World Wide Web at
http://www.harpercollins.com/paperbacks

96 97 98 99 ❖ 10 9 8 7 6 5 4 3 2 1

IT'S A WONDERFUL LIFE™

1

Snow was falling on the simple whitewashed sign that proclaimed in plain black letters:

YOU ARE NOW IN BEDFORD FALLS

Behind it, a banner draped with patriotic bunting read:

WELCOME HOME, HARRY BAILEY

Strings of colored Christmas lights shone against the early evening darkness. Heavy snow hushed the footfalls of the few people out and about and dampened the hiss of the cars advancing slowly along the streets. Bedford Falls was an ordinary town, the kind you'd see on Christmas cards or in a snow-dome in someone's parlor—a town like a thousand others, with ordinary houses and stores and sidewalks and people.

On this particular night, Bedford Falls was about to experience a miracle.

Like most miracles, it started with a prayer. One prayer, then another, and another, and another. The prayers from Bedford Falls that night went up for a man named George Bailey.

From Gower's Drugstore: "I owe everything to George Bailey. Help him, dear Father. . . ."

From Martini's bar and restaurant: "Joseph, Jesus, and Mary, help my friend, Mr. Bailey."

A mother's prayer: "Help my son George tonight. . . ."

And a cop on the beat: "He never thinks about himself, God. That's why he's in trouble."

From Bedford Falls Garage: "George is a good guy. Give him a break, God."

And from a nearby house, George's house, a young wife's voice: "I love him, dear Lord. Watch over him tonight."

Then a little girl's voice: "Please, God, something's the matter with Daddy."

And another child's voice: "Please bring Daddy back."

At that moment, an astronomer looking up at the starlit winter sky might have seen an odd flickering between two bright stars—brilliant, responsive flashes, as though the stars were in celestial dialogue.

"Hello, Joseph. Trouble?"

"Yes, Franklin. Looks like we'll have to send someone down. A lot of people asking for help for a man named George Bailey."

"George Bailey. Yes, tonight's his crucial night. You're right. We'll have to send someone down immediately. Whose turn is it?"

"That's why I came to see you, sir." The disdain in his voice was obvious. "It's that clockmaker's turn again."

"Oh—Clarence," Franklin said with a deep chuckle. "Hasn't got his wings yet, has he?"

"We've passed him up right along. Because you know, sir, he's got the IQ of a rabbit."

"Yes," Franklin replied with affection, "but he's got the faith of a child—simple. Joseph, send for Clarence."

A few moments later, something that looked like a shooting star streaked across the heavens. "You sent for me, sir?"

"Yes, Clarence," Franklin said. "A man down on Earth needs our help."

"Splendid!" Clarence exclaimed. "Is he sick?"

"No, worse," Franklin explained. "He's discouraged. At exactly ten forty-five P.M. Earth time, that man will be thinking seriously of throwing away God's greatest gift."

"Oh, dear, dear," Clarence cried. "His life? Then I have only an hour to dress. What are they wearing now?"

"You will spend that hour getting acquainted with George Bailey."

"Sir," Clarence asked hopefully, "if I should accomplish this mission, I mean, uh, might I perhaps win my wings? I've been waiting for over two hundred years now, sir—and people are beginning to talk."

Franklin paused thoughtfully. "What's that book you've got there?"

"*The Adventures of Tom Sawyer.*"

"Clarence," Franklin said, "you do a good job with George Bailey, and you'll get your wings."

"Oh, thank you, sir! Thank you!"

"Poor George," Joseph groaned, then instructed his charge, "Sit down."

"Sit down?" Clarence blurted out. "What are we—?"

"If you're going to help a man," Joseph said gruffly, "you want to know something about him, don't you?"

"Well, naturally. Of course."

"Well," Joseph ordered, "keep your eyes open." Joseph gazed down at the tiny spinning blue sphere its inhabitants called Earth, down through the clouds to the ground below.

"See the town?" Joseph asked.

Clarence squinted. "Where? I don't see a thing!"

"Oh, I forgot," Joseph sighed impatiently. "You haven't got

your wings yet. Now, look, I'll help you out. Concentrate. Begin to see something?"

"Why . . . yes! This is amazing!"

"If you ever get your wings, you'll see all by yourself."

"Oh, wonderful!" Clarence exclaimed.

2

Slowly, gradually, Clarence began to see a hillside where the deep snow had drawn a noisy crowd of boys. In the center of the group, a lanky, good-looking boy in a stocking cap and plaid coat shouted something through a megaphone; Clarence couldn't quite make out his words above the clamor.

The boy shook his hands over his head like a prizefighter, then straddled the blade end of a snow shovel as if it were a sled and gripped the wooden handle. "Okay, boys!" he shouted into the megaphone. "Let's go!"

Cheering and yelling, the boys gave the shovel-straddler a hard push—and then he was sliding down the hill, faster and faster, shouting exuberantly at the gathering speed and the cold air whipping his cheeks. He hit bottom and spun across the frozen pond below.

"Hey, who's that?" Clarence asked.

"That's your problem—George Bailey."

"A boy?"

They watched as George skidded to a stop, eyes shining, face flushed with the thrill of the ride.

"That's him when he was twelve, back in 1919," Joseph explained. "Something happens here you'll have to remember later on."

George scrambled up and dragged his shovel back to the snowy bank, yelling through his megaphone, urging his companions to give it a try. "Come on, Marty! Let's go!"

Marty zoomed down and spun to a stop on the frozen pond.

The next boy, brimming with bravado, skimmed down the hill, thumbs in his ears, wiggling his fingers in imitation of donkey's ears, braying, "Hee-haw, hee-haw!"

"Let's go, Sammy. Hee-haw!" George echoed, imitating his friend. A moment later he bellowed through the megaphone, "And here comes the scare-baby, my kid brother—Harry Bailey!"

"I'm not scared!" Harry proclaimed as, with some hesitation, he positioned himself on his shovel. If he was a little scared, he surely wouldn't let the older boys know it. Resolute, he pushed off, raising his mittened hands high in the air.

"Come on, Harry!" George and his friends shouted, urging the youngster on. "Come on, Harry!"

Harry reached bottom, but he didn't spin to a stop as the other boys had done. Perhaps the hill had grown more slippery, or perhaps he'd been going too fast; maybe he was just too scared to figure out how to control his descent. Unable to stop his makeshift sled, he sped straight across the pond through the thin-ice warning markers and plunged into the freezing water.

"Help, George, help!" Harry screamed.

The boys ran forward, slipping and sliding, struggling for footing on the slick ice, George in the lead, shouting, "Hang on, Harry, hang on!" Without a moment of hesitation, George was in the water, reaching for his brother. Seconds later, gasping, one arm clutching Harry, he ordered the others, "Chain, gang!"

His friends fell to their bellies, each holding on to the next boy's feet, forming a human chain back to solid ground. Slipping and tugging, they managed to haul George and Harry out of the icy water to safety.

At this point, the angel Joseph interjected, "George saved his brother's life that day. But he caught a bad cold, which infected his left ear. Cost him his hearing in that ear. It was weeks before he was able to go back to his after-school job at old man Gower's drugstore."

Joseph showed Clarence the events of the day George returned to work: the same band of boys on a warmer afternoon, sporting baseball caps, swinging bats and gloves, arms linked and whistling as they marched down the street. Suddenly they stopped, intimidated by the appearance of an old-fashioned, horse-drawn, stately black carriage making its way down the street among the cars. The boys stared, silent.

George pointed. "Mr. Potter!"

"Who's that?" Clarence asked in awe. "A king?"

Joseph shook his head. "That's Henry F. Potter, the richest and meanest man in the county."

The carriage passed. The youngsters returned to their light-hearted whistling. They crossed the street and, playing crack-the-whip, reached Gower's Drugstore, where they merrily flung George from the whip's end through the open doors.

A girl in a flowered dress, a big white bow in her hair, perched patiently on a stool at the soda fountain, smiling as she watched George skitter to a stop.

He walked directly to the smokes counter, where Mr. Gower kept a large wooden lighter for the convenience of his customers. In a private magical ritual, George placed his left forefinger over the lighter switch, closed his eyes, raised his right hand with fingers crossed, and made the same wish he always did: "Wish I had a million dollars."

He lifted his finger away and peeked at the lighter, where a small flame danced. A good omen, he thought. "Hot dog!"

Whistling, he marched behind the soda fountain to hang up his hat and coat. "It's me, Mr. Gower, George Bailey!" he called out cheerfully.

The old man peered through the frosted glass of the pharmacy section. "You're late!" he scolded.

Surprised and stung by the druggist's uncharacteristic sharpness, George simply answered, "Yes, sir."

He saw Mr. Gower move back a step and take a long swig from what appeared to be a bottle of whiskey. George frowned; that wasn't like Mr. Gower.

His thoughts were interrupted by the spirited appearance in the drugstore of a pretty girl with curly blond hair. She spotted the girl sitting at the counter and slid to a stop, frowning.

George was behind the fountain putting on his apron as she climbed onto a stool.

"Hello, George," she said brightly, then sighed, "hello, Mary."

Mary turned her back on the newcomer and, pretending boredom, looked around the store. "Hello, Violet."

"Two cents' worth of shoelaces?" George suggested Violet's usual candy purchase.

"She was here first," Violet said, nodding to Mary.

"I'm still thinking," Mary insisted.

"Shoelaces?" George asked again.

"Please, Georgie," Violet agreed, giving him her biggest smile.

George went to get the stringlike sweets, and both girls twirled on their stools, following him with their eyes.

Violet sighed. "I like him."

"You like every boy," Mary accused.

"What's wrong with that?"

George returned from the candy counter. "Here you are," he said, trading the paper sack of sweets for her pennies.

"Help me down?" Violet asked flirtatiously.

George made a face. "Help you down?" Indignant, he walked back behind the counter, shaking his head, to ring up her purchase. Mary grinned.

Violet jumped down off her perch and headed for the door. Leaning back with her elbows on the counter, Mary stuck out her tongue at Violet's retreating back.

"Made up your mind yet?" George asked Mary.

Mary turned around and smiled prettily at George. "I'll take chocolate."

"With coconut?" George asked as he started scooping ice cream into a dish.

"I don't like coconut," Mary said.

"You don't like coconut!" George said with disbelief. "Say, brainless, don't you know where coconuts come from?" He pulled a rolled-up magazine from his back pocket and laid it flat on the counter for Mary to see. "Lookit here—from Tahiti, the Fiji Islands, the Coral Sea!"

"A new magazine!" Mary exclaimed. "I never saw it before." She started to look at it, but he grabbed it back, pointing to the title, *The National Geographic Magazine*. "Of course you never. Only us explorers can get it." He jabbed his thumb into his chest and announced proudly, "I've been nominated for membership in the National Geographic Society!"

As George bent to scoop more ice cream, Mary leaned over the counter, her mouth near his left ear. "Is this the ear you can't hear in?" When George didn't answer, Mary whispered quickly, "George Bailey, I'll love you till the day I die."

Totally oblivious to Mary's words of love, George straightened up and gestured at her with the ice cream scoop. "I'm going out exploring someday, you watch. And I'm going to have a couple of harems, and maybe three or four wives. Wait and see."

Whistling again, he turned around and dumped several large spoonfuls of coconut onto the chocolate ice cream as Mary gazed at him in adoration.

"George! George!" Mr. Gower bellowed from his office.

The boy glanced toward his boss, alarmed. Mr. Gower was

a nice old man; it wasn't like him to yell that way. "Yes, sir?"

"You're not paid to be a canary!" Gower growled, clenching a cigar in his teeth.

"No, sir." Still holding Mary's sundae, George caught sight of a sheet of paper lying on the cash register—a telegram. He picked it up and read:

BEDFORD FALLS NY QAB 605 31 3EX MAY 3 1919 1211 AE

MR EMIL GOWER

BEDFORD FALLS NY

WE REGRET TO INFORM YOU THAT YOUR SON ROBERT DIED VERY SUDDENLY THIS MORNING OF INFLUENZA STOP EVERYTHING POSSIBLE WAS DONE FOR HIS COMFORT STOP WE AWAIT INSTRUCTIONS FROM YOU STOP

EDWARD MELLINGTON

PRESIDENT HAMMERTON COLLEGE

Slowly, George replaced the wrinkled telegram and stared at Mr. Gower. Somber now, he set the dish of ice cream in front of Mary and made his way to the back room.

"Uh, Mr. Gower, do you want something . . . anything?"

"No!" Mr. Gower snapped. Obviously drunk, the old man's hands were shaking as he filled some capsules with a powdery substance.

"Anything I can do back here?"

"No!" The pharmacist staggered, losing his balance and

scattering the capsules across the floor as he tried to steady himself.

"I'll get them, sir!" George quickly knelt to retrieve them.

Gower took his cigar from his mouth and, slurring his words, ordered, "Take those capsules over t' Miz Blaine's. She's waitin' for 'em."

"Yes, sir."

The old man tossed a small white box onto the counter and stumbled to an easy chair at the rear of his office. He sank wearily into the soft leather seat. Chewing on his cigar, head tilted back, he stared mournfully at a photograph of his son.

As George stood up from gathering the capsules he noticed the large glass jar of powder from which Mr. Gower had filled the prescription. Drug names and chemical formulas meant nothing to him, but he could clearly see that one side of the jar was marked POISON.

The boy stared at the jar, at the capsules in his hand, then at the druggist.

He walked gingerly to Gower's side. "They have the diphtheria there, haven't they, sir?"

"Mmm."

Still George lingered, looking this way and that, searching for a way to tell his boss that he might have made a mistake. "Is it a charge, sir?"

"Yes, charge," Gower whispered in the saddest voice George had ever heard. The man's eyes were glazed with tears. He seemed to be a million miles away.

The boy glanced at the bottle again. "Mr. Gower, I think—"

"Aw, get going!" Gower erupted, leaping from his chair and swatting at the boy with his arms.

George backed away. "Y-Yes, sir!"

Looking nervously at the box of lethal capsules in his hand, he pulled his cap down from the hook and yanked it on, wondering what to do. He glanced up, and the answer came to him from an advertising poster hanging above the smokes counter. It showed an elderly gentleman enjoying a smoke, with the caption:

ASK DAD.

HE KNOWS.

SWEET CAPORAL

Ask Dad. That was it! George dashed out and ran down the street, stopping only when he reached the building where a sign marked his father's business. It read:

BAILEY BROS.

BUILDING & LOAN

ASSOCIATION

Racing past the fancy horse and carriage parked on the street in front of the building, George sprinted up the steps to the office. The staff—Uncle Billy, Cousin Tilly, and Eustace—were huddled outside the closed door of his father's office, listening.

George reached for the knob, but his uncle Billy stopped him, his teacup rattling in its saucer. "Avast there, Captain Cook! Where you headin'?"

"Got to see Pop, Uncle Billy!"

"Some other time, George."

"It's important!"

Uncle Billy shook his head and moved the boy away from the door. "There's a squall in there that's shapin' up into a storm."

"Uncle Billy," Tilly called out. "Telephone."

"Who is it?"

"The bank examiner."

"Bank examiner!" The cup and saucer in his right hand clattered as he held up his left; he had forgotten the string tied around his forefinger and pinkie to remind him. "Oh! I should have called him yesterday! Switch it inside," he instructed as he hurried into his office and shut the door.

Seeing his chance, George ducked into his father's office. The elegantly dressed Mr. Potter sat in his wheelchair in front of Mr. Bailey's desk. They seemed to be arguing.

"I'm not crying, Mr. Potter—"

"Well, you're begging," Potter said. "And that's a whole lot worse."

"All I'm asking for is thirty days more."

George went around the desk to his father. "Pop—"

"Just a minute, son." Mr. Bailey turned back to Potter. "Just thirty short days. I'll dig up that five thousand somehow."

"Pop!"

"Shove me up, shove me up," Mr. Potter ordered the stone-faced bodyguard who always accompanied him. The man obediently moved the wheelchair closer.

"Have you put any real pressure on these people of yours to pay those mortgages?" Potter demanded.

"Times are bad, Mr. Potter. A lot of these people are out of work."

"Then foreclose!"

"I can't do that," Bailey insisted. "These families have children."

"Pop!" George said.

"They're not my children."

"But they're somebody's children, Mr. Potter."

The ruthless old man waved his hands in the air. "Are you running a business or a charity ward?"

"Well, all right—"

"Not with my money!"

"Mr. Potter," Bailey said, coming around to sit on the front edge of his desk, "what makes you such a hard-skulled character? You have no family, no children. You can't begin to spend all the money you've got."

"Oh," Potter said with a harsh laugh, "I suppose I should give it to miserable failures like you and that idiot brother of yours to spend for me."

"He's not a failure!" George protested, rushing toward Potter. "You can't say that about my father!"

"Shhh, George," his father said soothingly. "Be quiet, now."

"You're not!" George insisted. "You're the biggest man in town."

"Run along."

"Bigger'n him!" George shoved both hands into Potter's chest. "Bigger'n everybody!"

Mr. Bailey steered his son toward the door. Potter shrugged and sneered, "Gives you an idea of the Baileys!"

George looked up at his father and pleaded, "Don't let him say that about you, Pop!"

Bailey gently propelled the boy out the door. "All right, son, all right. Thanks. I'll talk to you tonight." He slipped back inside and closed the door. Within moments, the muffled sounds of arguing began again.

George turned to go, then remembered the small white pill-box in his hand. He hadn't had a chance to ask his father's advice. Now what?

George's feet felt like lead as he walked back to the drugstore. He didn't stop this time to make a wish on Mr. Gower's big old lighter. He didn't even see that little pest Mary, still sitting on the swivel stool at the fountain, waiting for him, watching him at first with adoration and then with a worried frown.

If only he could have talked to his father! Pop would have known what to do—he always did. All George knew was that he just couldn't deliver that medicine to Mrs. Blaine!

Just as the boy reached for the brim of his navy baseball cap to hang it on the brass hook of the hat rack, Mr. Gower's raspy shout startled him. He spun around.

In the back of the shop, the swaying pharmacist stood clutching the base and receiver of the black candlestick telephone. He sputtered into the mouthpiece, drink slurring his words.

"Wha—?" he shouted. "Why, tha' med'cine shoulda been there'n hour ago! It'll be over'n five minutes, Miz Blaine."

With some difficulty, Mr. Gower replaced the receiver and shoved the telephone onto the counter. Scowling and muttering, he turned, swaying, and spotted George.

"Where's Miz Blaine's box o' capsules?" the old man demanded.

George froze, eyes wide, his answer choking in his throat.

Gower stumbled forward and grabbed the boy by the front of his cotton shirt. Bottles of pills, powders, and liquids rattled on the wooden shelves as the enraged man dragged George to the back room.

"Didn' ya hear what I said?" he yelled into George's face, and the boy shrank from his boss's sour breath.

"Y-Yes, sir," George stuttered fearfully, "I—"

"What kinda tricks're ya playin', anyway?" Mr. Gower shouted, and slapped the boy hard across the left side of his face.

George struggled, but he couldn't get away. Gower was a slight man, and he was drunk, but he held on to George with the iron grip of an angry madman.

"Whyn't ya deliver 'em right away?" Gower raged, slapping the terrified boy again and again.

"You're hurting my sore ear!" George sobbed. A thick, dark stream of blood trickled from his bad ear down his cheek.

Watching silently from the soda fountain, Mary winced, too frightened to move or cry out.

"You lazy loafer!" Gower ranted on, venting his anger and grief on the child before him.

Unable to flee, unable to fight back, George's words finally came tumbling out. "Mr. Gower," he cried, "you don't know what you're doing! You put something wrong in those capsules. I know you're unhappy—you got that telegram, and you're upset. . . ."

As startled as if he'd been splashed with a bucket of cold water, Gower dropped his hold and gaped at the boy.

George could have run. Instead, hands shaking, shoulders hunched against another beating, he held out the small white box of pills.

"You put something bad in those capsules," he wept. "It wasn't your fault, Mr. Gower."

Trembling, the druggist snatched the box from the terrified boy's hands.

"Just look and see what you did," George went on, crying softly. He pointed to the tall, heavy glass bottle standing on the pharmacist's work counter. "Look at the bottle you took the powder from. It's poison! I tell you, it's poison!" George wiped his wet face, and his voice softened. "I know you feel bad. . . ."

Gower stared at the bottle, then at the black writing on the white label as if the word *poison* were written in a foreign language. With trembling fingers he slid open the tiny box, dug out a capsule, and broke it open, spilling its white contents into his palm. Breathing heavily, he dipped a fingertip into the powder, then touched it to the tip of his tongue.

The druggist's eyes widened in horror, and a harsh groan ripped from his throat as he grabbed the counter. He spun around and reached for George, his eyes wild.

George stumbled backward, sobbing, holding his arms in

front of his face to block another beating. "Don't hurt my sore ear again!" he pleaded.

"Oh, no . . . no, no, no . . . ," Mr. Gower said, grabbing for the boy.

"Don't hurt my sore ear again!"

The old man didn't strike George. He fell to his knees and took the boy's face in his hands. "Oh, George, George . . ." He hugged him fiercely.

George stopped struggling. He understood that his words had sliced their way through the alcohol and the grief. He threw his arms around the desolate man's neck, sobbing into his shoulder.

"Mr. Gower, I won't ever tell anyone," he cried fiercely. "I know what you're feeling. I won't ever tell a soul. Hope to die, I won't!"

Together they wept for Mr. Gower's dead son—and for the other life that most surely would have been lost if not for George Bailey.

3

A tall, thin, good-looking man in a suit and bow tie leaned over the store counter, a disappointed look on his face.

The clerk was holding up a small suitcase for his inspection. "An overnight bag. Genuine English cowhide, combination lock, fitted up with brushes, combs—"

"Nope, nope, nope. Now, look, Joe—I want a big one!" the other man emphasized, stretching his long arms wide apart . . . and froze.

Up in the heavens, Clarence asked, "What did you stop it for?"

"I want you to take a good look at that face," Joseph said.

"Who is it?"

"George Bailey."

"Oh, you mean the kid that had his ears slapped back by the druggist?"

"That's the kid."

Clarence studied the young man for a moment. "Ah, it's a good face. I like it. I like George Bailey. Tell me, did he ever tell anyone about the pills?"

"Not a soul."

"Did he ever marry the girl? Did he ever go exploring?"

"Well," Joseph said patiently, "wait and see."

As if in a movie reel that had stopped and restarted, George resumed talking and gesticulating. "Big. See, I don't want one for one night. I want something for a thousand and one nights, with plenty of room here for labels from Italy and Baghdad, Samarkand . . . a great big one."

Joe grinned. "I see. A flying carpet, huh?"

"Yeah."

Joe reached under the counter and brought up a huge brown leather suitcase. "I don't suppose you'd like this old second-hand job, would you?"

"Now you're talking!" George said. "Gee whiz, I could use that as a raft in case the boat sunk." He examined the bag from end to end. "How much does this cost?"

"No charge."

George shook his head and leaned forward. "That's my trick ear, Joe. It sounded like you said no charge."

"That's right," Joe said, grinning. He held the suitcase up to reveal the lettering stamped to the right of the handle: GEORGE BAILEY.

Surprised, George asked, "Well, what's my name doing on it?"

"A little present from old man Gower," Joe revealed. "Came down and picked it out himself."

"He did?" George exclaimed. "Well, whadya know about that! My old boss . . . isn't that nice."

"What boat you sailing on?" Joe asked.

"I'm working across on a cattle boat."

"A cattle boat?"

George shrugged and grinned. "Okay, I like cows."

George picked up the suitcase and headed for the drugstore, now a popular hangout for the local kids. The wide floor was occupied by white café tables, and the place reverberated with the happy sound of chattering youngsters.

George hurried over to his former boss and shook his hand. "Hello, Mr. Gower. Thanks ever so much for the bag. It's just exactly what I wanted."

"Aw, forget it."

"Oh, it's wonderful of you to think of me."

"Hope you enjoy it."

Just then George spotted the old cigarette lighter on the counter. He laid his left hand on the lighter, raised his right hand with his fingers crossed, and closed his eyes. "I wish I had a million dollars." He looked down as he snapped the light. "Hot dog!" he exclaimed at the tiny flame.

It was a beautiful day, and George felt wonderful. He started home. He had a small fortune saved up, a suitcase to pack, and a future stretching before him like an endless blue sky. At last he was going to leave this old two-bit town. He was going to see the world!

"Avast there, Captain Cook!"

As George passed his father's office building, Uncle Billy, Cousin Tilly, and Eustace waved to him from an upstairs window.

"You got your sea legs yet?" Billy asked.

"*Parlez-vous français,* mister?" Eustace hollered. "Hey, send us some of those picture postcards, will you, George?"

"Hey, George," Billy shouted, "don't take any plugged nickels!"

George laughed and waved and held up his big old suitcase for them to see. "Hey, George," Tilly joked, "your suitcase is leaking!"

"Hey, Ernie!" George hurried across the street to where his friend was sitting in his parked taxi. Bert the cop was there, too, leaning against the fender, reading a newspaper.

"Hey, I'm a rich tourist today. How about driving me home in style?" George said.

"Sure, Your Highness, hop in. And for the carriage trade"— Ernie reached inside and pulled on his cap—"I put on my hat."

George started toward the passenger door.

"Good afternoon, Mr. Bailey."

George, Ernie, and Bert swiveled toward the sound of the woman's voice.

"Hello, Violet." George looked her up and down. "Hey, you look good. That's some dress you got there."

Violet glanced down at the flowered summer dress that followed her every curve. "Oh, this old thing? Why, I only wear it when I don't care how I look." She fluffed her blond hair and grinned, then crossed the street as George, Bert, and Ernie watched wistfully. A man passing in the other direction nearly got run over as he gawked after her.

Ernie laughed. "How would you like—"

"Yes," George said, and hopped into the backseat.

Ernie grinned at Bert as he hung his head out the window. "Want to come along, Bert? We'll show you the town."

"No, thanks," Bert said, glancing at his wristwatch. "I think I'll go home and see what the wife's doing."

Ernie chuckled. "Family man."

That night the Baileys' fringed dining room chandelier swayed precariously over the food-laden table, jarred by the rambunctious carryings-on of the Bailey brothers on their last night together.

"George! Harry!" Mrs. Bailey shouted upstairs to them. Annie, their housekeeper and cook, pounded on the ceiling with a broom handle.

"You're shaking the house down," Mrs. Bailey went on. "Stop it!"

"Oh, let them alone," Mr. Bailey said good-naturedly from his place at the table. "I wish I was up there with them."

"Harry will tear his dinner suit!" his wife fumed. "George!"

"That's why all children should be girls," Annie announced firmly.

"But if they were all girls," Mrs. Bailey said, "there wouldn't be any . . . oh, never mind. George! Harry! Come down to dinner this minute," she called, climbing the stairs to their room.

"Everything's getting cold, and you know how long we've been waiting for you!"

"Okay, Mom," George hollered down.

Moments later Harry and George came down singing, carrying their mother seated on their arms between them as if she were a showgirl on a swing at the Ziegfeld Follies.

"Ta-da!"

Mrs. Bailey giggled as Annie and Mr. Bailey applauded and the dog raced around them, barking.

"Here's a present for you, Pop," George announced as the boys deposited their mom on his lap. She laughed and put her arms around him; Mr. Bailey kissed his wife's hand.

"Oh, you two idiots!" she protested, a smile and a blush belying her harsh words. "George, sit down and have dinner."

"I've eaten," said Harry.

"Well, aren't you going to finish dressing for your graduating party?" Mrs. Bailey asked. "Look at you!" Harry's tux collar was sticking up, and he was only half dressed.

"I don't care," Harry said with a shrug. "It's George's tux." He turned toward Annie, flinging open his arms. "Annie, my sweet, have you got those pies?" he asked, playfully chasing her around the table.

"If you lay a hand on me," she squealed, grinning, "I'll hit you with this broom."

"Annie," Harry teased as he followed her through the swinging door into the kitchen, "I'm in love with you. There's a moon tonight!"

Laughing, George also sat down. He patted his ribs as he surveyed the delicious dinner set out in front of him. "Boy, oh, boy. My last meal in the old Bailey boardinghouse."

"Oh, my lands, my blood pressure!" Mom said, fanning herself as she plopped into her seat at the table.

"Pop," Harry said from the kitchen door, "can I have the car? I'm going to take over a lot of plates and things."

"What plates?" Mrs. Bailey exclaimed.

"Oh, Mom, I'm chairman of the eats committee, and we only need a couple of dozen."

"Oh, no, you don't, Harry. Now, not my best Haviland," Mrs. Bailey cried, hurrying after him into the kitchen.

"Oh, let him have the plates, Mother," George said.

George and his father ate in comfortable silence for a moment.

"Hope you have a good trip, George," Mr. Bailey said finally as he held out a plate of muffins. "Uncle Billy and I are going to miss you."

"I'm going to miss you, too, Pop." George reached for a muffin and, looking up, noticed that his father looked pale and drawn. "What's the matter? You look tired."

"Oh, I had another tussle with Potter today."

"Oh . . ."

"I thought when we put him on the board of directors, he'd ease up on us a little bit."

George dug into his dinner. "What's eating that old money-grubbing buzzard, anyway?"

"Oh, he's a sick man. Frustrated and sick. And his mind's sick, and his soul—if he has one. He hates everybody that has anything that he can't have. Hates us mostly, I guess."

George's muttered response was cut off as Harry came through the swinging door, a pie in each hand and one on his head, his mother behind him. "Gangway! Gangway! So long, Pop."

"You got a match?" George teased.

Harry rolled his eyes. "Very funny, very funny."

"Put those things in the car and I'll get your tie and studs ready for you," Mrs. Bailey said. "Hurry up. Don't you drop those!"

"Okay, Mom." Harry glanced at George. "You coming later?"

"What do you mean?" George joked. "And be bored to death?"

"Couldn't want a better death," Harry said with a wink. "Lots of pretty girls, and we're going to use that new floor tonight, too."

"Oh, I hope it works," George said.

"No gin tonight, son," Mr. Bailey added.

"Aw, Pop, just a little?"

"No, son. Not one drop."

"Aw," Harry complained as he headed out the door.

"Boys and girls and music," Annie muttered, serving slices of pie around the table. "Why do they need gin?"

"Father," George asked around a mouthful of food, "did I act like that when I graduated from high school?"

"Pretty much. You know, George, I wish we could send Harry to college with you. Your mother and I talked it over half the night."

"Oh, but we have that all figured out," George said. "You see, Harry'll take my job at the building and loan and work there four years, then he'll go."

"He's pretty young for that job," Mr. Bailey said.

"No younger than I was."

"Well, you were born older, George," Mr. Bailey said softly.

George hadn't quite caught that, as Mr. Bailey was sitting on his left, the side of his bad ear. "How's that?"

"I said you were born older," Mr. Bailey repeated more loudly, then added, "I suppose you've decided what you want to do when you get out of college."

"Oh, well, you know what I've always talked about. Build things. Design new buildings. Plan modern cities . . . all that stuff I was talking about."

"Still after that first million before you're thirty?"

"No, I'll settle for half of that in cash."

Annie came in to serve coffee.

"Of course, it's just a hope, but, uh . . . you wouldn't consider coming back to the building and loan, would you?" Mr. Bailey said, putting down his fork to look directly at George. On George's other side, Annie set his coffee down and leaned over, listening for his answer.

George nearly choked on his food. His bow tie suddenly felt too tight. "Well, I . . ." He poked at the food on his plate a moment, then felt Annie bending over his shoulder, listening expectantly. Glancing up, he teased, "Annie, why don't you draw up a chair? Then you'd be more comfortable, and you could hear everything that's going on."

Annie straightened and swaggered off in a huff. "I would if I thought I'd hear anything worth listening to!"

"You would, huh?" George winked at his dad.

The humorous interlude had eased the tension a little, giving George time to recover from the shock of his father's suggestion. But Mr. Bailey persisted. "I know it's too soon to talk about it—"

"Oh, no, no, Pop, I—" George squirmed a little in his seat. "I couldn't. I couldn't face being cooped up for the rest of my life in a shabby little office."

His father glanced up, eyebrows raised, and when George realized the insult he'd just paid, he blushed.

"Oh, I'm sorry, Pop, I didn't mean it that way, but it's this business of nickels and dimes and spending all your life trying to figure out how to save three cents on a length of pipe. I'd go crazy. I want to do something big and something important."

Mr. Bailey nodded, then added quietly, "You know, George, I feel that in a small way we're doing something important. Satisfying a fundamental urge. It's deep in the race for a man to want his own roof and walls and fireplace, and we're helping him get those things in our shabby little office."

"I know, Pop." George pushed his chair back, feeling miserable. "I wish I felt, uh . . . but I've been hoarding pennies like a miser here in order to . . . most of my friends have already finished college. I just feel like if I didn't get away, I'd bust!"

"Yes, yes. You're right, son." But the disappointment showed plainly on Mr. Bailey's face.

"You see what I mean, don't you, Pop?"

Mr. Bailey propped his elbows on the table, rubbing his hands together, a look of resignation on his features. "This town is no place for any man unless he's willing to crawl to Potter. And you've got talent, son. I've seen it." He managed a smile. "You get yourself an education. Get out of here."

George stared at his plate a moment. "Pop, you want a shock?" he asked softly. "I think you're a great guy." His father looked momentarily surprised, then rewarded his son with a tired smile.

Annie, peering through the glass window of the kitchen door, was listening intently. George looked at her. "Oh, did you hear that, Annie?"

"I heard it!" she hollered, moving away from the door. "About time one of you lunkheads said it."

George grinned. "I'm gonna miss old Annie." But his father didn't respond. He stared blindly at his plate, his mouth set in a grim line, his mind elsewhere—perhaps at the building and loan, where it usually was.

George knew he was disappointing the old man, but there was no getting around it; the truth had to be told. He couldn't come back to Bedford Falls, he just couldn't, no matter what anyone said or did. The whole world lay before him, and George was busting loose, running for it with open arms. Life was far too wonderful to spend it rotting away in a stuffy second-floor office in this poor excuse for a town. His father had made his choice, and George was sorry if he had regrets. But this was George's life they were talking about now, and he'd be damned if he'd miss his chance.

His father would get used to the idea, sooner or later. He'd have to. That's all there was to it.

Appetite gone, George tossed down his napkin and shoved away from the table. "Pop, I think I'll get dressed and go over to Harry's party."

Mr. Bailey nodded absently, not looking up. "Have a good time, son."

George promised himself that he would—just as soon as he got out of town.

4

The Bedford Falls High School graduation dance was in full swing when George arrived. He made his way through the crowd to the refreshment table, where Harry introduced him to some of his friends. "You know my kid brother, George," he joked. "I'm going to put him through college."

A classmate of Harry's stuck out his hand. "Hello, George."

Just then George spotted an old pal. The young man greeted George in a familiar way: thumbs in his ears and wiggling his fingers. "Hee-haw!"

George laughed, delighted. "Sam Wainwright! How are you? When did you get here?"

Sam was beaming. "Oh, this afternoon. I thought I'd give the kids a treat."

"Old college graduate now, huh?"

"Yeah, Old Joe College Wainwright, they call me." Playfully, Sam plucked George's necktie out of his jacket. "Well, freshman, it looks like you're going to make it after all." He grinned. Unlike George, Sam hadn't had to delay his college education.

"Yep." Harry took the ribbing in stride—it was just Sam's way. As George looked down to rearrange his tie Sam noticed Harry.

"Hello, Sam."

"Harry! You're the guy I want to see. The coach has heard all about you!"

"He has?"

"Yeah. He's followed every game, and his mouth's watering. He wants me to find out if you're going to come along with us."

Harry shrugged. "I've got to make some dough first."

"Well, you'd better make it fast," Sam advised him. "We need great ends like you—not broken-down old guys like this one." He gestured at George, grinning.

Sam had them all laughing when Mr. Partridge, the school principal, squeezed in.

"George, welcome back," he hailed.

"Hello, Mr. Partridge. How are you?" George shouted over the noise. Mr. Partridge was old, but he had a youthful enthusiasm for new ideas. His latest point of pride was the newly installed gym floor—a modern marvel that could retract at the touch of a button to uncover an Olympic-size swimming pool below.

"Putting a pool under this floor was a great idea. Saved us another building. Now, Harry, Sam, have a lot of fun. There's lots of stuff to eat and drink. Lots of pretty girls."

As if on cue, Violet appeared. "Boys, I've got one third of my dance card left," she announced. She turned to George and smiled seductively. "What am I bid?"

"Hello, Violet," George said.

"George!" It was Marty Hatch, pressing through the crowd toward George like a man on a mission.

"Hiya, Marty!" George shook Marty's hand. "Well, it's old home week!"

"Do me a favor, will you, George?" Marty pleaded.

"What's that?" George said.

"Well, you remember my kid sister, Mary?"

"Oh, yeah, yeah," George acknowledged.

Sam stuck his head in. "'Mama wants you, Marty! Mama wants you.' Remember?"

The guys all laughed.

"Dance with her, will you?" Marty pleaded.

"Oh . . . me?" George squirmed. "Oh, well, I feel funny enough already, with all these kids."

"Aw, come on. Be a sport. Just dance with her one time, and you'll give her the thrill of her life."

Sam egged him on. "Aw, go on!"

"Hey, sis!" Marty yelled.

Violet pouted.

"Well . . . excuse me, Violet," George mumbled. He'd do it as a favor for his old pal Marty, but he sure hoped the band would play a short one. "But don't be long," he complained. "I don't want to be a wet nurse for . . ."

George looked over the crowded room for the brainless, skinny little pest he remembered from Gower's Drugstore. He saw that Marty had stopped to talk to someone else, a lovely girl with a radiant smile. Freckle-faced Freddy was obviously trying to make time with her, but though she was listening politely, he wasn't getting anywhere.

George stopped dead and stared at her.

The girl felt his gaze and looked up. Their eyes met.

George was stunned. A slow smile spread over his face. That was Mary? Little Mary Hatch?

She was beautiful—as pretty as a sunrise on an April morning, as fresh and delicate as a flower.

And he was going to dance with her. George made a beeline for her; after all, he'd promised his old pal Marty, right? What were friends for?

"And the next thing I know," Freddy was saying to Mary as George approached, "some guy came up and tripped me."

Mary had barely moved, but her smile had widened and her eyes were on George.

"That's the reason why I came out in fourth," Freddy persisted. "If it hadn't been for that, that race would have been a cinch. I tried to find out who it was later, but I couldn't find out. Nobody'd ever tell you whoever it was because they'd be scared. They know what kind of a—"

"You remember George!" Marty barged in. "George, this is Mary." His duty done, big brother made a quick getaway. "Well, I'll be seeing you."

"Well, well, well . . . ," George heard himself say feebly.

"Now to get back to my story," Freddy continued, trying hard to hold the girl's attention.

But Mary had already floated into George's arms as the band began a lilting version of "Buffalo Gals."

"Hey!" Freddy griped. "This is my dance!"

"Oh, why don't you stop annoying people?" George scolded over his shoulder.

"Well, I'm sorry," Freddy apologized without thinking. Then, "Hey!"

George turned back to Mary and whirled her off into the crowd of dancers. "Well, hello," he finally thought to say.

"Hello," Mary said back. George seemed bewildered. "You look at me as if you didn't know me."

"Well, I don't," George admitted.

"You've passed me on the street almost every day!" Mary challenged him.

"Me?"

"Uh-huh."

"Uh-uh." George shook his head. "That was a little girl named Mary Hatch. That wasn't you."

Suddenly the music stopped. Harry Bailey jumped onto the bandstand.

"Oyez, oyez, oyez," he announced into the microphone. "This is the big Charleston contest!"

The crowd cheered.

"The prize," Harry continued, "a genuine loving cup! Those not tapped by the judges will remain on the floor!" he finished. "Let's go!"

The band and the dancers got right to it. Spotlights played over the action on the floor.

"I'm not very good at this," George warned Mary.

Mary laughed. "Neither am I."

"Okay! What can we lose?"

They joined the mob of dancers. The pounding of dancing feet reverberated as the crowd got into full swing and the pace grew more frenzied.

"You're wonderful!" George yelled over the noise. He put his heels together and crossed his hands as he flapped his knees, with Mary dancing circles around him.

Freddy, meanwhile, was moping by the stairs, behind the bars of the metal handrail. A friend, Mickey, also partnerless, strolled over to him.

"What's the matter, Othello?" he kidded Freddy. "Jealous?"

Freddy shrugged.

Mickey's voice took on a sly, confidential tone. "Did you know there's a swimming pool under this floor?" he asked, which of course Freddy did.

"And did you know that button behind you causes this floor to open up?" he went on.

Freddy still wasn't interested.

"And did you further know that George Bailey is dancing right over that crack?" Mickey continued.

That got Freddy's attention. "But what about—"

Mickey grinned. "I've got the key."

The scorned lover snatched it away and turned it in the lock.

The mechanism rumbled. The floor started to part like two geologic plates along a fault line, but smoothly and silently.

The band never stopped playing as the gap widened.

Dancers screamed, leaping the chasm to safety on either side of the expanding moat. Soon the whole assemblage stood packed along the sidelines.

Everyone except George Bailey and Mary Hatch.

They had no idea that the floor behind them was gone as they danced backward to the edge.

"Whooooaaaah!" the crowd roared when Mary and George switched directions at the last possible second.

"They're cheering us!" George shouted to Mary. "We must be pretty good!"

Back they went again—and over the side they fell. The splash was tremendous. What a finale! The crowd loved it.

George and Mary came up for air, looking around to see what had happened. Everyone was cheering. What else could they do but keep on dancing, waist deep in the middle of the pool?

Inspired by their example, other couples plunged in, fully dressed, like seals flinging themselves into the sea. Freddy and Mickey jumped in, too.

Even Mr. Partridge couldn't resist. "Oh, well," he sighed, and leaped in, leaving his faculty members behind, wide-eyed.

It was one swell party.

When it was over, George and Mary, wearing dry garments borrowed from the locker room, met outside and set off down a narrow lane where hydrangea blooms lay heavy along a white picket fence in the moonlight. Still damp, Mary was draped in a white Bedford Falls High School warm-up robe. George had on a striped football jersey and padded football pants several sizes too big.

As they walked, Mary sang, "Buffalo gals, can't you come out tonight, can't you come out tonight, can't you come out tonight. Buffalo gals, can't you come out tonight . . . "

They faced each other to harmonize on the last line: "And dance by the light of the moon." They were terrible.

"Oh, hot dog. Just like an organ," George lied.

"Beautiful." Mary laughed.

They continued walking, Mary carrying her wet clothes in a bundle.

"I told Harry I thought I'd be bored to death," George remembered. "You should have seen the commotion in that locker room. I had to knock down three people to get this stuff we're wearing. Here, let me . . . let me hold that wet dress of yours."

Mary stopped. "Do I look as funny as you do?" she asked.

George hitched his pants up. "I guess I'm not quite the football type," he joked. Then, "You . . . you look wonderful."

Mary blushed and resumed walking.

George hoped she wasn't offended. "You know," he called after her, "if it wasn't me talking, I'd say you were the prettiest girl in town."

Mary stopped. "Well, why don't you say it?"

What kind of question was that? George wondered as he hurried to catch up. "I don't know," he said uncomfortably. "Maybe I will say it." And maybe he wouldn't. "How old are you, anyway?" he wanted to know.

"Eighteen," Mary told him.

"Eighteen . . . why, it was only last year you were seventeen!"

"Too young or too old?" Mary wondered.

George thought he'd said the wrong thing again. "Oh, no, no. Just right. Your age fits you! Yes, sir," George stumbled along, "you look a little older without your clothes on—I mean, without a dress. You look . . . older. I mean, younger. You look just—"

He accidentally stepped on the trailing belt of her robe, jerking her to a stop.

"Sir, my train, please," she said, affecting a courtly manner.

"A pox upon me for a clumsy lout," George played along, and laid the belt over her arm. "Your . . . your caboose, my lady," he said.

"You may kiss my hand."

They were very close. George felt his face flushing.

"Um, hey . . . hey, Mary . . . "

Mary turned away shyly, singing softly. "As I was lumbering down the street . . . "

"Okay, then," George had an idea. "I'll throw a rock at the old Granville house."

"Oh, no, don't," Mary pleaded. "I love that old house."

George was surprised. "No, you see, you make a wish and then try and break some glass. You got to be a pretty good shot nowadays, too." It was true; most of the panes were gone.

"Oh, no, George, don't. It's full of romance, that old place. I'd like to live in it."

"In that place?"

"Mmm-hmmm."

"I wouldn't live in it as a ghost," he said. "Now watch. Right on the second floor, there. See?"

George hurled a rock at the house.

Crash! The pane disappeared, and glass tinkled inside.

"What'd you wish, George?" Mary wondered when it was quiet again.

"Well, not just one wish. A whole hatful," George exclaimed. "Mary, I know what I'm going to do tomorrow and the next day and next year and the year after that. I'm shaking the dust of this crummy little town off my feet and I'm going to see the world—Italy, Greece, the Parthenon, the Coliseum. Then I'm coming back here and going to college and see what they know. And then I'm going to build things. I'm gonna build airfields. I'm gonna build skyscrapers a hundred stories high."

Mary stooped and picked up a rock.

"I'm gonna build a bridge a mile long—" He stared at her

watching the old house. "What, are you gonna throw a rock?"

She hauled off and threw.

Crash! Bull's-eye.

"Hey, that's pretty good! What'd you wish, Mary?"

"Buffalo gals, can't you come out tonight, can't you come out tonight, can't you come out tonight?" she sang, evading his question.

"What'd you wish when you threw that rock?" George asked again.

"Oh, no," she said.

"Come on, tell me."

"If I told you, it might not come true."

"What is it you want, Mary? What do you want? You want the moon? Just say the word, and I'll throw a lasso around it and pull it down. Hey, that's a pretty good idea. I'll give you the moon, Mary."

"I'll take it," Mary said. "Then what?"

George imagined Mary holding the moon. "Why, then you could swallow it, and it'd all dissolve, see? And the moon-beams'd shoot out of your fingers and your toes and the ends of your hair." He looked into her eyes. "Am I talking too much?"

"Yes!" shouted a man from the balcony of a neighboring house.

They turned in shock and looked up.

"Why don't you kiss her instead of talking her to death?" the man complained. He was roughly the age of George's father. He'd been up there in his rocking chair the whole time.

"How's that?" George asked.

"Why don't you kiss her instead of talking her to death?" he repeated loudly, annoyed.

George looked at Mary, then back at the old guy. "Want me to kiss her, huh?"

The man rose from his chair, positively disgusted. "Aw, youth is wasted on the wrong people!" he griped as he went inside and slammed the door behind him.

"Hey, hey, hold on," George protested. "Hey, mister, come on back out here."

Mary tugged at his arm, shaking her head.

"I'll show you some kissing that'll put hair back on your head!" George threatened. "What are you—"

At that moment Mary shrieked and ran off.

When George turned, he noticed that Mary had disappeared. He looked at the ground and jumped. Her robe lay in a heap on the sidewalk. The belt was trapped under George's foot again.

"Mary?" he said as he picked up the robe.

No answer.

"Okay, I give up. Where are you?"

"Over here in the hydrangea bushes," she confessed.

George took the robe over. "Here you are," he said. "Catch." He started to toss the robe, then stopped. "Wait a minute. What am I doing?" He paced around the bushes. "This is a very interesting situation."

The bushes shook violently. "Please give me my robe!" Mary demanded.

"Hmmm." George was thinking aloud. "A man doesn't get into a situation like this every day," he observed.

"I'd like to have my robe," Mary insisted.

"Not in Bedford Falls, anyway."

Mary sneezed.

"Gesundheit," George replied, and picked up where he'd left off. "This requires a little thought here."

"George Bailey!" Mary scolded. "Give me my robe!"

"I've heard about things like this, but I've never—"

"Shame on you," Mary snapped. "I'm going to tell your mother on you."

George thought about that. "Oh, my mother's way up the corner there," he said helpfully.

"I'll call the police!" Mary shouted.

"They're way downtown," George reminded her. "They'd be on my side, too."

"Then I'm going to scream!" Mary yelled. Her angry movements in the bushes were scattering petals everywhere.

"Maybe I could sell tickets," George said, thinking out loud. "Let's see . . . no, the point is, in order to get this robe—I've got it! I'll make a deal with you, Mary—"

Headlights suddenly appeared around the corner, and a black car skidded to a halt in front of George. Harry was behind the wheel, and Uncle Billy was leaning out the side.

"George! George!" he gasped.

George tossed the robe across the bushes and hurried over to the car.

Uncle Billy was distraught. "George! Come on home, quick! Your father's had a stroke."

George was stunned. "Mary . . . Mary," he called out toward the hydrangea bushes. "I'm sorry. I've got to go."

"Come on, George, let's hurry!" Harry ordered.

"Did you get a doctor?" George asked as he clambered into the backseat.

"Yes," Harry answered.

"Campbell's there now," Uncle Billy said as the car raced off down the street.

Mary rose from the bushes, pulling the robe close. All of a sudden she felt a chill.

5

"I think that's all we'll need you for, George. I know you're anxious to make a train." Dr. Campbell, chairman of the board of the Bailey Brothers Building and Loan Association, stood up at the head of the conference room table.

Beside him, George rose, putting papers into a folder. "I have a taxi waiting downstairs."

"I want the board to know that George gave up his trip to Europe to help straighten things out here these past few months," Campbell said. He shook George's hand and smiled. "Good luck to you at school, George."

The men around the table added their good wishes.

"Now we come to the real purpose of this meeting," Campbell went on as George gathered up his things. "To appoint a successor to our dear friend Peter Bailey."

"Mr. Chairman," Henry Potter interrupted, "I'd like to get to my real purpose."

"Wait just a minute now—" one of the board members began.

"Wait for what?" Potter spat. "I claim this institution is not necessary to this town. Therefore, Mr. Chairman, I make a motion to dissolve this institution and turn its assets and liabilities over to the receiver."

Uncle Billy jumped from his chair and slammed his fist on the table. "Potter, you dirty . . . I'll wring his neck! George, you hear what that buzzard—"

Everyone began arguing at once. Dr. Campbell pounded his gavel, trying to quiet the uproar.

"Mr. Chairman," a board member said indignantly, "it's too soon after Peter Bailey's death to talk about chloroforming the building and loan!"

"Peter Bailey died three months ago," another member countered. "I second Mr. Potter's motion."

"Very well," Campbell agreed, though reluctantly. "In that case, I'll ask the two executive officers to withdraw."

Billy got up to leave with George.

"But before you go," the chairman added, "I'm sure the whole board wishes to express its deep sorrow at the passing of Peter Bailey."

"Thank you very much," George said softly.

"It was his faith and devotion that are responsible for this organization," Campbell added.

"I'll go further than that," Potter chimed in loudly. "I'll say that to the public, Peter Bailey *was* the building and loan."

Billy leaned forward angrily. "Oh, that's fine, Potter, coming from you, considering that you probably drove him to his grave!"

"Peter Bailey was not a businessman. That's what killed him. Oh, I don't mean any disrespect to him, God rest his soul. He was a man of high ideals—so-called. But ideals without common sense can ruin this town."

George's distaste for the man showed clearly on his face. He was only too glad to be getting out of this town, away from Potter. He wasn't going to listen to any more of Potter's self-important drivel—he didn't have to. He slipped toward the door.

"Now, you take this loan here to Ernie Bishop," Potter went

on, picking up a folder of papers. "You know," he sneered, "that fellow that sits around all day on his, er, brains in his taxi, you know."

George had retrieved his coat and was at the door, but he paused at the mention of his friend's name.

"I happen to know the bank turned down this loan," Potter ranted, incredulous, "but he comes here, and we're building him a house worth five thousand dollars! Why?"

"Well, I handled that, Mr. Potter," George spoke up. "You have all the papers there—his salary, insurance. I can personally vouch for his character."

Potter smiled sarcastically. "A friend of yours."

"Yes, sir."

"You see?" Potter asserted, as if his point had been proven. "If you shoot pool with some employee here, you can come and borrow money." He chuckled condescendingly. "What does that get us? A discontented, lazy rabble instead of a thrifty working class. And all because a few starry-eyed dreamers like Peter Bailey stir them up and fill their heads with a lot of impossible ideas. Now, I say—"

"Just a minute, just a minute," George interrupted, making his way back to his place at the table. "Now hold on, Mr. Potter. You're right when you say my father was no businessman. I know that. Why he ever started this cheap penny-ante building and loan, I'll never know. But neither you nor anybody else can say anything against his character, because his whole life was . . . why, in the twenty-five years since he and Uncle Billy started this thing, he never once thought of himself. Isn't that right, Uncle Billy? He didn't save enough money to send Harry to school, let alone me."

Potter folded his hands, rolling his eyes toward the ceiling as if bored.

"But he did help a few people get out of your slums, Mr. Potter," George went on. "And what's wrong with that?" He appealed to the men seated around the table. "Why, you're all businessmen here. Doesn't it make them better citizens? Doesn't it make them better customers? You . . . you said they . . . what'd you say just a minute ago? They had to wait and save their money before they even thought of a decent home? Wait? Wait for what?" George demanded, his voice rising. "Until their children grow up and leave them? Until they're so old and broken-down that they . . . do you know how long it takes a working man to save five thousand dollars?"

Potter stifled a yawn.

"Just remember this, Mr. Potter, that this rabble you're talking about, they do most of the working and paying and living and dying in this community. Well, is it too much to have them work and pay and die in a couple of decent rooms and a bath? Anyway, my father didn't think so," George declared, his voice breaking. "People were human beings to him, but to you—a warped, frustrated old man—they're cattle. Well, in my book, he died a much richer man than you'll ever be."

"I'm not interested in your book," Potter snarled. "I'm talking about the building and loan."

"I know very well what you're talking about," George snapped. "You're talking about something you can't get your fingers on, and it's galling you. That's what you're talking about, I know."

George straightened up, realizing he'd perhaps gone too far, gotten too involved. He looked around uneasily at the board members staring silently at him. "Well, I've said too much. I . . . you're the board here. You do what you want with this thing. There's just one thing more, though. This town needs this measly, one-horse institution, if only to have someplace where people can come without crawling to Potter." Angrily, he grabbed his papers and coat and headed for the door. "Come on, Uncle Billy."

Potter didn't answer; he sat there for a moment, almost as if he was stunned that anyone would dare talk to him—or about him—that way. The board members, too, sat speechless—until the door slammed behind George and Billy.

Potter shook his head. "Sentimental hogwash. I want my motion acted on—"

The boardroom erupted into a heated discussion.

In the outer office, Billy crowed, "Boy, oh, boy, that was telling him, George old boy. You shut his big mouth. You should have heard him!" he told the office staff.

George put his files away and donned his hat and coat without answering. He looked troubled.

"What happened?" Eustace asked. "We heard a lot of yelling."

"Well," Billy said, "we're being voted out of the business after twenty-five years. Easy come, easy go."

Tilly shook her head and snatched up the newspaper. "Well, here it is: 'Help Wanted. Female.'"

Just then Ernie, his cab waiting outside for George, poked his head in the doorway. "You still want me to hang around, George?"

"Yeah, I'll be right down."

"Hey, you'll miss your train," Billy said, giving George a gentle push. "You're a week late for school already. Go on!"

But George couldn't bring himself to leave. He kept looking back at the boardroom. "What's going on in there?"

"Oh, never mind. Don't worry about that," Billy said. "They're putting us out of business. So what? I can get another job. I'm only fifty-five."

"Fifty-six," Tilly corrected.

"Go on, go on. Hey, look, you gave up your boat trip. Now, you don't want to miss college, too, do you?"

Campbell came rushing out of the office. "George! George! They voted Potter down! They want to keep it going!"

"Whoopee!" Billy shouted as Tilly and Eustace cheered and danced around.

That was all George needed to hear. Relieved, he quickly said his good-byes and grabbed his suitcase.

"You did it, George, you did it!" Campbell crowed. "But they've got one condition—only one condition."

The employees of the salvaged Bailey Brothers Building and Loan Association fell silent.

George felt his stomach lurch. "What's that?"

"That's the best part of it," Campbell said, beaming. "They've appointed George here as executive secretary to take his father's place."

"Oh, no!" George exclaimed. "But Uncle Billy—"

"You can keep him on," Campbell assured him. "That's all right. As secretary, you can hire anyone you like."

"Dr. Campbell, now, let's get this thing straight," George said, brimming with anger and frustration. "I'm leaving. I'm leaving here right now. I'm going to school. This is my last chance. Uncle Billy here—he's your man."

He grabbed his suitcase and strode to the office door—to his escape from this small, crummy town and this pitiful, measly business, to the door that opened to his future. All he had to do was keep walking, keep going, through that portal, and he'd be out of there, heading for the fulfillment of his dreams.

"But George," Campbell pleaded, "they'll vote with Potter otherwise."

George froze at the threshold, his face twisted in agony, recognizing that the door to his future had just slammed shut, as tight as any tomb.

6

"I know, I know," Clarence muttered. "He didn't go."

"That's right," Joseph answered. "Not only that, but he gave his school money to his brother, Harry, and sent him to college. Harry became a football star. Made second team All-American."

"Yeah," Clarence said impatiently. "But what happened to George?"

"George got four years older waiting for Harry to come back and take over the building and loan."

George paced impatiently, eagerly, hands stuffed casually into his pockets, in front of the Bedford Falls train station. Uncle Billy sat on a bench eating peanuts from a paper sack. It was a warm spring day, and George was in a wonderful mood because his brother, Harry, was coming home on the next train—a genuine college graduate. George had missed him, to be sure, but it was more than that. Harry's homecoming meant that finally, after a long and painful four-year wait slaving away at the Bailey Brothers Building and Loan Association, it was George's turn for freedom, for adventure.

"Oh, there are plenty of jobs around for somebody who likes

to travel," he told Billy with enthusiasm. He dug a fistful of brochures from his suit pocket and shuffled through them like a deck of cards. "Lookit this here—Venezuela oil fields: 'Wanted. Man with construction experience.' Here's the Yukon, right here: 'Wanted. Man with engineering experience.'"

George whirled around at the sound of a train whistle and gazed down the tracks, a look of pure joy on his face.

"There she blows! You know what the three most exciting sounds in the world are?"

His uncle nodded. "Breakfast is served; lunch is served; dinner—"

"No, no, no," George said with a grin. "Anchor chains, plane motors, and train whistles."

"Peanut?" Billy offered, holding up the bag.

As the train pulled into the station and passengers began to disembark, George and Billy hurried over to find Harry.

"There's the professor now," George announced.

Harry jumped down from the train, and he and George both started talking at once as they shook hands and pummeled each other on the back.

"Old Professor Phi Beta Kappa Bailey, All-American!"

"Well, if it isn't old George Geographic Explorer Bailey," Harry teased back. "What? No husky dogs? No sled? Uncle Billy, you haven't changed a bit."

Billy grinned. "Nobody ever changes around here. You know that."

"Oh, am I glad to see you!" George cried.

"Where's Mother?" Harry asked, looking around.

"She's home, cooking the fatted calf." George put his arm around his brother and started herding him toward the car. "Come on, let's go."

"Oh, wait, wait! Wait a minute!" Harry said, and turned back to the train.

A young blond woman wearing a stylish traveling suit, a pert hat with veil, and a corsage had been hovering behind them on the train steps. She burst into a radiant smile the moment Harry laid eyes on her. Holding out his hand, he led her down the steps and over to his family, grinning broadly. "George, Uncle Billy, I want you to meet Ruth."

Somewhat startled, slightly confused, George removed his hat and smiled politely. Pretty girl, he thought. "Hello."

"Ruth Dakin," Harry added, slipping his arm around her.

The girl pretended to be insulted. "Ruth Dakin Bailey, if you don't mind."

George's face fell.

"Huh?" Billy blurted.

"Well, I wired you I had a surprise," Harry said sheepishly. "Here she is. Meet the wife."

"Well, what do you know," Billy gushed. "Wife!"

Harry and Ruth grinned, glancing expectantly back and forth between the two men.

Recovering, George shook hands formally with his new sister-in-law. "Well, how do you do? Congratulations." Then the news sank in. "What am I doing? Congratulations!" he shouted. "They're married, these two!" He pumped Ruth's hand up and down and kissed her on the cheek, then shoved Harry's hat down on his head. "Why didn't you tell somebody?"

As they began walking down the platform George and Uncle Billy flanked their new relative, badgering her with questions.

"Are you really married?" Billy asked.

"Why, yes," Ruth giggled.

"Hey, what's a pretty girl like you doing marrying this two-headed brother of mine?" George joked.

"Well, I'll tell you, it was purely mercenary," she joked back. "My father offered him a job."

Harry stopped; his smile vanished.

"Oh, he gets you *and* a job?" Billy gushed, walking on with her. "Well, Harry's cup runneth over."

Harry winced and came up behind his brother, placing a hand on his shoulder. "George, about that job . . . Ruth spoke out of turn. I never said I'd take it. You've been holding the bag here for four years, and . . . well, I won't let you down, George. I would like to—" Harry grabbed his hat. "Oh, wait a minute! I forgot the bags. I'll be right back."

George stared after him a long moment, his mind spinning. It couldn't be happening again. Not again.

He caught up with Uncle Billy and Ruth, where they were surrounded by friends being introduced to the new bride.

Ruth offered him some of the popcorn the enthusiastic Billy had insisted on buying for her from a vendor. "Here, have some popcorn, George."

Dazed, he took some but didn't eat it.

"George, George, George," Ruth chattered on prettily. "That's all Harry ever talks about."

"Ruth, uh, this . . . what about this job?" George had to know.

"Oh. Well, my father owns a glass factory in Buffalo. He wants to get Harry started off in the research business."

"Well, uh, is it a good job?"

"Oh, yes, very. Not much money, but a good future, you know. Harry's a genius at research. My father just fell in love with him."

"And you did, too."

Ruth's smile said it all.

There was a big party at the Bailey house that night to celebrate Harry and Ruth's marriage.

"Oh, boy, oh, boy, oh, boy," Uncle Billy said to George, having rejoiced with a bit too much to drink. "I feel so good, I could spit in Potter's eye." His eyes lit up behind his wire-rimmed glasses. "In fact, I think I will!"

George leaned against the porch column, chuckling. Poor Uncle Billy, he thought affectionately; the old guy was quite a hoot on a good day. That night he looked like a drunken teddy bear.

"Whadya say? Huh?"

George grinned and shook his head.

"Oh, maybe I'd better go home. Where's my hat?" Alarmed, he looked around the porch. George plucked the missing hat from his uncle's head and held it out.

"Oh, thank you, George." He stared for a moment at the blurred images before his eyes, squinting. "Which one's mine?"

"The middle one," George assured him with a grin.

"Oh, thank you, George old boy. Now, look, if you'll point me in the right direction—will you do that, George?" He laughed and slapped his nephew on the shoulder. "Old building-and-loan pal, huh?"

George patted his uncle on the back and maneuvered him down the porch steps. "Now, you just turn this way and then go right straight down there."

"That way, huh?" Uncle Billy took off, singing, "My wild Irish rose . . . "

Crash! He collided with the neighbor's trash cans.

George winced.

"I'm all right, I'm all right," Uncle Billy called out, and went on singing. "The sweetest flower that grows . . . "

George smiled and headed back toward the house. He stood outside, struck a match on the steps, and lit a cigarette. Inhaling, he strolled back to the front gate and leaned against the post, letting the gentle sounds of laughter and dance music waft over him in the cool night air. A train whistle moaned on its way out of town. George listened wistfully, filled with longing.

Glancing down, he noticed the corner of a brochure sticking out of his inside coat pocket. He pulled out the colorful advertisements he'd shown Uncle Billy, with their beautiful pictures and dazzling words, their glossy pages full of promises.

Europe, South America . . . "Travel with the Foremost Student Tours College Travel Club" . . . who was he kidding? Angrily, he flung the enticing brochures into the gutter.

Footsteps coming from the house made him turn.

"Oh, hello, Ma."

She looked so pretty that night, her dark hair pulled back and shining, dressed up in a flowing spring frock and pearls, the lines on her face erased by her glowing smile. She looked happier than he'd seen her since before his father's death.

Barely as tall as his shoulder these days, even in heels, she reached up and pulled his face down for a kiss, then patted his chest. "That's for nothing," she said softly. She smiled and snuggled into the arm he wrapped around her shoulders, then tipped her head back toward the house. "How do you like her?"

"Oh, she's swell, isn't she?"

His mother grinned knowingly. "Looks like she can keep Harry on his toes."

"Keep him out of Bedford Falls, anyway," George muttered.

Mrs. Bailey bent her head to hide the pained look that crossed her face. Then she smiled. "Did you know that Mary Hatch is back from school?"

"Mmm-hmmm."

"Came back three days ago."

"Mmm-hmmm."

"Nice girl, Mary."

"Mmm-hmmm."

"Kind that will help you find the answers, George."

"Mmm-hmmm."

"Oh, stop that grunting," his mother chided.

He shrugged quizzically. "Hmmm?"

"Can you give me one good reason why you shouldn't call on Mary?"

"Sure. Sam Wainwright."

"He—?"

"Yeah, Sam's crazy about Mary."

"She's not crazy about him," Mrs. Bailey asserted.

"Well, how do you know? Did she discuss it with you?"

"No . . ."

"Well, then, how do you know?"

"I've got eyes, haven't I? Why, she lights up like a firefly whenever you're around."

George made a face. "Aw . . ."

"And besides, Sam Wainwright's away in New York, and you're here in Bedford Falls."

"And all's fair in love and war."

She grinned mischievously. "I don't know about war. . . ."

George laughed and hugged his mother affectionately. "Mother of mine, I can see right through you—right to your back collar button. Trying to get rid of me, huh?"

She grinned. "Mmm-hmmm."

He kissed her, and she plopped his hat on his head. "Well, here's your hat, what's your hurry?"

George muttered. The little schemer had had his hat all along, he thought wryly, her intentions as clearly mapped out as a battle plan. George straightened his hat and sauntered out the gate. "All right, Mother, old building-and-loan pal, I think I'll go out and find a girl and do a little passionate necking."

His mother chuckled softly. "Oh, George . . ."

He took a drag on his cigarette. "Now, if you'll just point me in the right direction . . ."

She grabbed his upper arms and turned him sharply left, facing up the street toward Mary's house.

"This direction," George verified.

Beaming, Mrs. Bailey gave him a gentle shove of encouragement. George took a few steps, turned abruptly around, and, tipping his hat to his mother, strode off rapidly in the opposite direction. "Good night, Mrs. Bailey."

His mother stood watching, perplexed, as George headed for town.

7

It was a pleasant night for a stroll. In downtown Bedford Falls, friends and neighbors were out for no reason other than to share the sidewalk. George took the slightly more adventurous route, down the tree-lined median, off the beaten track, as was his way.

Violet had no trouble spotting him. She had two suitors already at her side—the kind of young men she attracted as easily as the streetlamps above attracted moths.

"Excuuuse me," she said, drawing out her words, her eyes on George.

"Now, wait a minute," one of her swains protested.

"I think I've got a date," Violet mused, parting her companions as though they were on hinges. "But stick around, fellas, just in case, huh?"

"We'll wait for you, baby," said the other, the mustachioed one.

Violet ran to catch up with George. "Hello, Georgie Porgie!" she called.

"What?" He stopped. What was Violet doing out in the middle of the street?

"What gives?" Violet said brightly.

George thought for a second. "Nothing," he admitted.

Violet hooked her arm under George's and walked him along. "Where are you going?" she asked sweetly.

"Oh, I'll probably end up down at the library."

"Georgie," Violet said impatiently, "don't you ever get tired of just reading about things?"

George stopped. "Yes!" She was right! He didn't want to read about things—he wanted to *do* things! Exciting things! "What are you doing tonight?" he demanded.

"Not a thing," Violet cooed.

"Are you game, Vi? Let's make a night of it!"

Now they were getting somewhere, Violet thought. "Oh, I'd love it, Georgie. What'll we do?" George looked as though he were ready to paint the town, dance until dawn, or shoot the works.

"Let's go out in the fields and take our shoes off and walk through the grass!" he said instead.

Violet was stunned. "Huh?"

"Then we can go up to the falls," he continued. "It's beautiful up there in the moonlight, and there's a green pool up there, and we can swim in it. Then we can climb Mount Bedford and smell the pines and watch the sunrise against the peaks, and we'll stay up there the whole night, and everybody'll be talking, and there'll be a terrific scandal—"

"George, have you gone crazy?" she cut him off angrily. Clearly, she found it an outrageous idea. "Walk in the grass in my bare feet?"

George suddenly became aware that they had drawn a small crowd—everyone laughed. George winced.

"Why, it's ten miles up to Mount Bedford!" Violet complained loudly.

"Shhh . . ." At that moment, ten miles away from town in any direction sounded pretty good to George.

"You think just because you—"

"Okay!" George snapped. "Just forget about the whole thing." He jammed his hands into his pockets and marched off, followed by the amused laughter of the crowd.

He walked down the quiet street, dragging a stick along the picket fences until he reached a mailbox lettered J. W. HATCH. The flag was out of place, and with nothing better to do, he paused to whack it back.

He ran the stick farther along the fence, then turned around and ran it back again.

A window opened on the second floor of the Hatch house, and Mary looked out.

"What are you doing, picketing?" she wanted to know.

George looked up, wearing a surprised expression. "Hello, Mary. I just happened to be passing by."

"Yes, so I noticed. Have you made up your mind?"

"How's that?"

"Have you made up your mind?"

"About what?"

"About coming in. Your mother just phoned and said you were on your way over to pay me a visit."

That was odd, George thought. "My mother just called you? Well, how did she know?" he asked.

"Did you tell her?" Mary asked.

"I didn't tell anybody. I just went for a walk and happened to be passing by."

Mary left the window and went into the hallway. "I'll be downstairs, Mother," she said.

"All right, dear."

Mary paused at the landing to check her hair. She dashed into the parlor, took a cartoon drawing out of the portfolio leaning against the table, and propped it conspicuously on the music stand. At the phonograph by the front door, she gave the record a spin and started the music. She opened the front door, smiling brightly.

"Well, are you coming in or aren't you?"

George gave the front gate a push, but it didn't open. He tried the latch; it seemed stuck, so he gave it a wiggle. It still didn't open. He wiggled it again; the gate still refused to give way. Frustrated, he kicked it open with a bang.

"Well, I'll come in for a minute," George said. "I didn't tell anyone I was coming over here, you know." After a moment he added, "When did you get back?"

"Tuesday," Mary said.

They stood in the doorway, close together. George removed his hat.

"Where'd you get that dress?" he asked.

"Do you like it?"

"It's all right," he mumbled. They stepped inside.

"I thought you'd go back to New York like Sam and Angie and the rest of them," he remarked as they stood in the foyer.

"Oh, I worked there a couple of vacations," Mary said. "But I don't know, I guess I was homesick."

George frowned. "Homesick? For Bedford Falls?"

"Yes, and my family, and . . . oh, everything. Would you like to sit down?" Mary motioned toward the parlor.

"All right, for a minute." He followed her in. "I still can't understand it, though. I didn't tell anybody I was coming here."

"Would you rather leave?" Mary asked.

"No, I don't want to be rude."

"Well, then, sit down."

George caught sight of the cartoon drawing on the music stand. It was a caricature of him as a cowboy, lassoing the moon.

"Some joke, huh?" he said.

George planted himself in the middle of the loveseat; Mary perched on the end.

"Well, I see it still smells like pine needles around here," George observed.

"Thank you," Mary responded.

Thinking he might remember the harmonizing they'd done on their walk after the graduation dance, she sang, "And dance by the light—"

"What's the matter?" George cut her off. Then he remembered the song: "Buffalo Gals." "Oh, yeah . . . yeah," he acknowledged. He checked the time on his wristwatch. "Well, I—" He moved to get up.

"It was nice about your brother, Harry, and Ruth, isn't it?" Mary interrupted him.

"Oh . . . yeah, yeah, that's all right," George admitted, fingering his hat.

"Don't you like her?"

"Well, of course I like her. She's a peach."

"Oh. Just marriage in general you're not enthusiastic about, huh?"

"No. Marriage is all right for Harry and Marty and Sam and you." George wasn't sure what he meant by that.

Mrs. Hatch called from the top of the stairs. "Mary! Mary! Who's down there with you?"

"It's George Bailey, Mother."

"George Bailey? What's he want?"

"I don't know." She turned to George. "What do you want?"

"Me? Not a thing." George dropped his hat on the small table and stood up. He jammed his hands into his pockets. "I just came in to get warm."

Mary cupped one hand around her mouth and called out, "He's making violent love to me, Mother!"

Mrs. Hatch answered instantly. "You tell him to go right back home, and don't you leave the house, either!" In a sweeter, persuasive tone, she added, "Sam Wainwright promised to call you from New York tonight."

George couldn't believe what Mary had told Mrs. Hatch. "But your mother needn't . . . you know I didn't come here to . . ."

"What did you come here for, then?" Mary stood up and confronted him.

"I don't know!" George snapped. "You tell me. You're supposed to be the one that has all the answers. You tell me."

"Why don't you go home?" Mary hissed angrily.

"That's where I'm going," George stated. "I don't know why I came here in the first place. Good night."

"Good night!"

George left. As the door slammed behind him he heard the telephone start to ring.

"Mary! Mary! The telephone! It's Sam!" called Mrs. Hatch.

"I'll get it!"

"Whatever were you doing that you couldn't hear?" her mother scolded.

Mary threw back the needle arm of the phonograph and picked up the record—"Buffalo Gals." She slammed it down furiously, shattering it.

"Mary!" Mrs. Hatch cried. The telephone was still ringing. "He's waiting!"

Mary picked up the receiver. "Hello?"

There was a quick knock at the door, and George let himself in.

"I forgot my hat!" He marched into the parlor to get it.

Mary forced herself to put on a happy face. "Hee-haw!" she said merrily. "Hello, Sam, how are you?"

Sam's voice came over the line. "Aw, great. Gee, it's good to hear your voice again."

"Well, that's awfully sweet of you, Sam. There's an old friend of yours here. George Bailey."

"You mean old mossback George?"

"Yes, old mossback George."

"Hee-haw. Put him on!"

George was still outside the door.

"Wait just a minute. I'll call him . . . George!"

Mrs. Hatch rushed downstairs. "He doesn't want to speak to George, you idiot!"

"He does so. He asked for him," Mary told her mother. "Geo—" she called, but he was already there; Mary nearly ran into him.

Mrs. Hatch marched back up the stairs and sat down on the landing to listen.

"George! Sam wants to speak to you," Mary told him.

He picked up the receiver. "Hi, Sam."

"Well, George Baileyoffski! Hey, a fine pal you are. What're you trying to do? Steal my girl?" In his New York office, Sam grinned at the young lady in the white fur stole who was rubbing his shoulder.

"What do you mean?" George replied indignantly. "Nobody's trying to steal anybody's girl. Here . . . here's Mary."

"No, wait a minute. Wait a minute. I want to talk to both of you. Tell Mary to get on the extension."

"Here. You take it. You tell him," George said to Mary.

"Mother's on the extension," Mary said.

"I am not!" Mrs. Hatch yelled from the top of the stairs.

Mary held the receiver where George could hear it, too. "We can both hear." To George: "Come here." They stood very close. "We're listening, Sam."

"I have a big deal coming up that's going to make us all rich. George, you remember that night in Martini's bar when you told me you read someplace about making plastics out of soybeans?"

A man in Sam's office wondered aloud, "Jelly beans?"

"Shut up!" Sam snapped. He continued into the phone, "Out of jelly—out of soybeans?"

"Huh? Yeah, yeah." George remembered, vaguely. "Soybeans. Yeah." Mary's nearness distracted him.

"Well, Dad snapped up the idea. He's going to build a factory outside of Rochester. How do you like that?"

"Rochester? Well, why Rochester?" George wondered.

"Why not? Can you think of anything better?"

"Oh, I don't know," George answered. "Why not right here? You remember that old tool and machinery works? You tell your father he can get that for a song. And all the labor he wants, too. Half the town was thrown out of work when they closed down."

"That so? Well, I'll tell him. Hey, that sounds great. Oh, baby, I knew you'd come through. Now, here's the point. Mary . . . Mary, you're in on this, too. Now, listen. You got any money?"

"Money?" George thought about it. "Yeah. Well, a little." He couldn't take his eyes off Mary—so close, so lovely.

"Well, now listen," Sam went on. "I want you to put every cent you've got into our stock, you hear? And George, I may have a job for you—that's unless you're still married to that broken-down building and loan. This is the biggest thing since radio. And I'm letting you in on the ground floor. And Mary . . . "

Mary was staring into George's eyes. "I'm here," she whispered into the phone.

"Would you tell that guy I'm giving him the chance of a lifetime, you hear? The chance of a lifetime."

Mary repeated it for George. "He says it's the chance of a lifetime."

George dropped the phone and grabbed Mary, trembling, shaking her, not knowing why, at war with his own emotions. "Now you listen to me," he told her. "I don't want any plastics. I don't want any ground floors. And I don't want to get married—ever—to anyone. You understand that?"

Mary was crying, but she didn't pull away.

"I want to do what I want to do," George sped on. "And

you're . . . and you're . . ." And then he was holding her, kissing her, pressing her close. "Oh, Mary . . . Mary . . ."

"George . . . George . . . George . . ."

Mrs. Hatch saw what was happening. Speechless and defeated, she ran to her room as George and Mary kissed, passionately, desperately, recklessly in love.

8

"Here they come!" Tilly shouted over the noisy assembly.

The strains of Handel's "Wedding March" followed George and Mary as they made their way down the rain-splashed steps of the church and through the festive crowd. Dodging showers of rice and rain, they ran to the curb and clambered into Ernie's waiting cab.

Mrs. Bailey smiled through her tears. "First Harry, now George. Annie, we're just two old maids now."

The Baileys' maid tossed her head. "You speak for yourself, Mrs. B.!" she teased.

Once Ernie had put some distance between them and the noisy wedding crowd, he eyed the happy couple in his rearview mirror. They were kissing, in a world of their own.

Ernie couldn't resist. "If either of you two sees a stranger around here, it's me!"

"Hey, look!" George exclaimed in mock surprise. "There's somebody driving this cab!"

Ernie grinned and passed a ribbon-wrapped bottle of champagne over the seat back. "Bert the cop sent this over. He said to float away to Happyland on the bubbles."

George accepted it gladly. "Look at this—champagne!"

Mary smiled. "Good old Bert."

Ernie was enjoying the company of the happy couple. "By the way," he chatted, "where are you two going on this here honeymoon?"

"Where're we going?" George exclaimed. "Look at this. There's the kitty, Ernie." George thumbed through a stack of bills as if it were a deck of cards. "Here, come on, count it, Mary."

"I feel like a bootlegger's wife. Look!" Mary held the money tightly, as if it might disappear.

"You know what we're going to do?" George said. "We're going to shoot the works. A whole week in New York, a whole week in Bermuda. The highest hotel, the oldest champagne, the richest caviar, the hottest music, and the prettiest wife."

George kissed Mary as Ernie whooped, "Then what?"

George couldn't think. "Then what, honey?"

"After that, who cares?"

"That does it! Come here!" George pulled Mary close.

The cab had reached downtown Bedford Falls. Something peculiar was happening. A steady stream of pedestrians was splashing through the rain ahead of them, crossing the street beneath the cover of black umbrellas. Ernie pulled the cab over and stopped at the corner. The people were in a hurry—and they were headed for the building and loan.

"Don't look now," Ernie warned, "but there's something funny going on over there at the bank, George."

A noisy crowd jammed the entrance to the Bailey Brothers Building and Loan Association.

"I've never really seen one," Ernie added, hoping he was wrong, "but that's got all the earmarks of being a run."

A pal of Ernie's running by spotted the cab and skidded to a stop long enough to gasp, "Hey, Ernie, if you got any money in the bank, you better hurry!"

Gripped by a premonition, Mary wanted to leave, to drive away quickly, before whatever it was ruined their perfect day. "George, let's not stop. Let's go!"

George regarded the mob with a mixture of concern and curiosity. "Just a minute, dear. Uh-oh . . . "

"Please, let's not stop, George."

George patted her arm, but his eyes were on the trouble in the street. "I'll be back in a minute, Mary."

He jogged across the puddled road and slowed to a walk as he approached the bottleneck at the entrance to the building and loan. The few townspeople who noticed him looked wary.

"Well, hello, everybody. Mrs. Thompson, how are you? Charlie . . ." George managed to appear calm, but he felt a sense of anxiety as he fumbled for his keys. "What's the matter here? Can't you get in?" Without a reply, the crowd made room for him to unlock the security gate, then herded in behind him.

George swung through the front office doorway, past the counter where Uncle Billy's pet crow was perched, and stopped, astonished, as he saw his uncle taking a long swallow of courage from a pint flask. George didn't want to believe it.

"What is this, Uncle Billy? A holiday?"

"George . . ." But Billy didn't want to say it.

George turned his attention to the customers who were packing the small lobby. "Come on in, everybody. That's right. Just come on in." He swept the crow out of the way and hurdled the low counter that separated the clerical and customer areas. He faced the crowd.

"Now look, why don't you all sit down? There are a lot of seats over there. Just make yourselves at home."

That seemed to settle them momentarily.

"George, can I see you a minute?" Billy said, retreating into his office.

George followed and shut the door. "Why didn't you call me?"

"I just did, but they said you left. This is a pickle, George. This is a pickle."

George confronted his uncle. "All right, now, what happened? How did it start?"

"Well, how does anything like this ever start? All I know is the bank called our loan."

"When?"

"About an hour ago. I had to hand over all our cash."

"All of it?"

"Every cent of it, and it still was less than we owe."

"Holy mackerel!"

"And then I got scared, George, and closed the doors. I . . . I . . . I . . ."

The phone rang, and Billy went to get it. George stepped over to the window and looked down on the street. "The whole town's gone crazy," he mused.

"Yes, hello?" Billy listened for a moment, then pressed the mouthpiece against his lapel. "George, it's Potter."

George answered without emotion. "Hello."

"George," Mr. Potter said, "there is a rumor around town that you closed your doors. Is that true?"

It didn't take long for word to get around a town like Bedford Falls. Nor did it take long for a man like Potter to pounce on the opportunity.

"No, sir."

"Oh. Well, I'm very glad to hear that," Potter said quickly. "George, are you all right? Do you need any police?"

"Police?" George exclaimed. "What for?"

Potter felt himself gaining the upper hand. "Well, mobs get pretty ugly sometimes, you know, George. I'm going all out to help in this crisis. I've just guaranteed the bank sufficient funds to meet their needs. They'll close up for a week and then reopen."

George held the phone aside and informed his uncle, "He

just took over the bank." With a sinking feeling, he realized that Potter was turning Bedford Falls into his personal chess game.

"I may lose a fortune," Potter went on, "but I'm willing to guarantee your people, too. Just tell them to bring their shares over here, and I will pay fifty cents on the dollar."

George knew that Potter's so-called generosity would ensure the demise of the Bailey Brothers Building and Loan Association.

"Aw, you never miss a trick, do you, Potter?" George said angrily. "Well, you're going to miss this one."

"If you close your doors before six P.M.," Potter warned, "you'll never reopen."

But George was finished talking. The click of the phone as he hung up startled Potter.

George studied the large photograph of his father hanging on his office wall. Defending the building and loan against Potter had never been easy, but Peter Bailey had always managed. What would he do in a situation like this? George wished he could ask him. He wondered if he had the strength to do it alone.

Billy wanted only to change the subject. "George, was it a nice wedding?" he asked shyly. "Gosh, I wanted to be there."

"Yeah," George said. He smiled weakly and looked at the string tied around his uncle's fingers. "You can take this one off now," he said.

George went to face the customers. He looked out at them through the cashier's window.

What could he say to these people who had trusted him with their hard-earned money? They were waiting expectantly, counting on him to say the words that would make things right. They needed him to give them answers that would reassure them their savings were secure.

"Now, just remember," George said hesitantly, his voice

cracking, "that this thing isn't as black as it appears." The words sounded leaden.

The room went dead silent. Mercifully, sirens in the street broke the spell as the crowd turned to the windows to see what was happening. When they turned back to George, he was ready.

"I have some news for you folks," George said matter-of-factly. "I've just talked to old man Potter, and he's guaranteed cash payments at the bank. The bank's going to reopen next week."

"But George, I've got my money here," Ed called out.

"Did he guarantee this place?" Charlie asked.

"Well, no, Charlie," George said slowly. "I didn't even ask him. We don't need Potter over here."

That was enough for Charlie. "I'll take mine now," he said simply.

"No, but you . . . you . . . you're thinking of this place all wrong," George reasoned, holding up his hands. "As if I had the money back in a safe." He looked directly into the eyes of his friends and neighbors, hoping his calm words would remind them of the reason the building and loan existed. "The money's not here." He pointed to the man nearest him. "Your money's in Joe's house—that's right next to yours. And in the Kennedy house, and Mrs. Macklin's house, and a hundred others. Why, you're lending them the money to build, and then they're going to pay it back to you as best they can. Now, what are you going to do?" George asked. "Foreclose on them?"

An old customer named Tom was unconvinced. "I got two hundred and forty-two dollars in here, and two hundred and forty-two dollars isn't going to break anybody."

"Okay, Tom. All right. Here you are." George produced a banking slip. "You sign this. You'll get your money in sixty days."

"Sixty days!"

Again George tried to explain. "Well, now, that's what you agreed to when you bought your shares."

"Tom! Tom!" A man named Randall pushed through the crowd to ask his friend, "Did you get your money?"

"No."

"Well, I did," Randall said. "Old man Potter'll pay fifty cents on the dollar for every share you got."

"Fifty cents on the dollar?" someone yelled.

"Yes—cash!"

The room exploded into debate about the merits of taking Potter up on his offer. After all, fifty cents on the dollar was better than losing your shirt!

"Well?" Tom asked George. "What do you say?"

"Now, Tom," George argued reasonably, "you have to stick to your original agreement. Now, give us sixty days on this."

Tom turned abruptly and called out to his friend, "Okay, Randall."

Mrs. Thompson clutched Tom's arm. "Are you going to go to Potter's?"

Tom shrugged. "Better to get half than nothing."

Others nodded and called out their agreement; the crowd moved toward the door.

George was losing them! "Tom!" George shouted, leaping over the counter. "Tom, Randall—wait!" He shoved through the crowd, struggling to reach the door. If they stormed out this way now, he'd lose them, lose them all. When he felt his hand on the doorknob, he closed the door softly but firmly, then turned and stood in front of it, begging for their understanding, commanding their attention with the pure, anguished sincerity of his words.

"Now, listen . . . now, listen to me. I beg of you not to do this thing. If Potter gets hold of this building and loan, there'll never be another decent house built in this town. He's already got charge of the bank, he's got the bus line, he's got the department stores, and now he's after us. Why? Well, it's very simple. Because we're cutting in on his business, that's why. And because he wants to keep you living in his slums and paying the kind of rent he decides."

Part snake-oil salesman, part preacher now, George pointed to one of his more recent customers in the crowd. "Joe, you had one of those Potter houses, didn't you?"

Joe nodded.

"Well, have you forgotten? Have you forgotten what he charged you for that broken-down shack? Here, Ed—you know. You remember last year when things weren't going so well, and you couldn't make your payments?"

Ed bent his head, eyes downcast.

"You didn't lose your house, did you?"

The man shook his head briefly.

"Do you think Potter would have let you keep it?" George turned to the crowd, his voice rising, pleading with them to listen to reason. "Can't you understand what's happening here? Don't you see what's happening? Potter isn't selling. Potter's buying! And why? Because we're panicky and he's not—that's why. He's picking up some bargains."

George's voice softened as he tried to rein in his panic. "Now, we can get through this thing all right. We've got to stick together, though. We've got to have faith in each other."

"But my husband hasn't worked in over a year," Mrs. Thompson argued, "and I need money!"

"How am I going to live until the bank opens?" another woman called out.

More worried voices called out their concerns—and they were legitimate concerns, difficult to argue with, for George himself well knew how hard it could be to make ends meet in times like these.

"I got doctor bills to pay!"

"I need cash!"

"I can't feed my kids on faith!"

"How much do you need?" A cheerful voice broke in above the hubbub.

Mary! George turned to her. He'd completely forgotten his new bride, hadn't even realized she'd followed him into the building—and now there she was, smiling just as brightly as the sun on a spring morning and holding up a handful of cash.

Their wedding cash. A gift beyond measure.

George could have kissed her right there in front of everybody. What was it his mother had said not so long before about Mary's having all the answers?

"Hey!" he called out exuberantly as hurried back behind the counter to his wife. He took her gift and held it high. "I've got two thousand dollars. Here's two thousand dollars! This'll tide us over till the bank reopens!" He moved to the cashier's window as his customers crowded around, with Tom heading up the line. "All right, Tom, how much do you need?"

"Two hundred and forty-two dollars," Tom said firmly.

"Aw, Tom," George groaned, "just enough to tide you over till the bank reopens."

"I'll take two hundred and forty-two dollars," Tom insisted.

George sighed and counted out the man's money. "There you are."

"That'll close my account."

George shook his head emphatically. "Your account's still here. That's a loan. Okay." Then he turned to the next customer. "All right, Ed."

"I got three hundred dollars here."

"Aw, now, Ed, what'll it take till the bank opens? What do you need?"

"Well," the man grumbled, "I suppose twenty dollars."

"Twenty dollars. Now you're talking!" George counted out the bills. "Fine! Thanks, Ed. All right now, Mrs. Thompson, how much do you want?"

The woman's face twisted in concern. "But it's your own money, George."

"Never mind about that. How much do you want?"

She thought a moment, then decided. "I can get along with twenty all right."

"Twenty dollars."

"And I'll sign a paper," she stated, her head held high.

"You don't have to sign anything. I know you'll pay it back when you can. That's okay." He looked at the next customer. "All right. Mrs. Davis?"

The tiny old lady peered timidly up at George, her voice tentative. "Could I have seventeen-fifty?"

"Seven—?" George reached across the counter, took Mrs. Davis's face in his hands, and kissed her soundly. The crowd laughed, and George felt the panic level in the room subside. "Bless your heart! Of course you can have it. You got fifty cents?"

And so George talked and joked his way through the afternoon, anxiously watching his pile of bills grow smaller and smaller. At last the Bailey Brothers Building and Loan office was empty save for George, Uncle Billy, Eustace, and Tilly, all eyeing the second hand of the big old clock on the wall as it clicked around the Roman numerals toward six o'clock.

"We're going to make it, George!" Uncle Billy giggled. "They'll never close us up today."

George called out the numbers as if counting down the minutes till midnight on New Year's Eve: "Six . . . five . . . four . . . three . . . two . . . one . . . bingo! We made it! Close the door, Eustace!" he shouted, and Eustace slammed and locked it. "Look, look, we're still in business," George crowed, holding up his last two dollar bills. "We've still got two bucks left."

Billy sighed and uncapped his bottle of whiskey.

"Well, let's have some of that! Let's celebrate," George

exclaimed. "Get some glasses, Tilly." George put his arm around his uncle. "We're a couple of financial wizards!"

"Those Rockefellers—ha!" Billy scoffed.

"Get a tray for these two great, big, important simoleons," George ordered as Tilly poured them each a drink.

"We'll save them for seed," Billy agreed, and raised his glass. "A toast!"

"A toast!" George seconded. "A toast to Mama Dollar and to Papa Dollar." He dropped the two singles into the wire basket Eustace held, then leaned over and sternly informed the bills, "And if you want to keep this old building and loan in business, you'd better have a family really quick."

"I wish they were rabbits," Tilly joked.

"I wish they were, too," George agreed.

They drank to that wish.

"Okay," George announced grandly, "let's put 'em in the safe and see what happens." The basket raised high, they paraded around the office, belting out "The Stars and Stripes Forever" before locking the meager treasure in the vault.

"Folks, folks," Eustace called out merrily. "Wedding cigars!"

"Uh-oh! Wedding! Holy mackerel, I'm married! Where's Mary? Mary . . ." But Mary wasn't in the office; when had she left? He glanced frantically at his watch.

"Poor Mary. Look, I've got a train to catch," he told the others, but stopped halfway to the door. "Well, the train's gone. I wonder if Ernie's still here with his taxicab."

"George," Tilly called out, "there's a call for you."

"Look, will you get my wife on the phone?" George asked, grabbing his coat. "She's probably over at her mother's."

Tilly shook her head. "Mrs. Bailey is on the phone."

"I don't want Mrs. Bailey. I want my wife"—and then it dawned on him. "Mrs. Bailey! Oh, that *is* my wife! Here, I'll take it in here." He ran to his office and grabbed the phone.

"Mary! Hello? Listen, dear, I'm sorry, I . . . What? Come

home? What home? . . . Three-twenty Sycamore? Well, what—whose home is that?" His eyebrows shot up. "The Waldorf Hotel, huh?"

George left the building and loan, turned up his collar against the driving rain, and hurried to Sycamore Street. He had the sneaking suspicion that he knew where he was going to wind up. His steps slowed as he neared the address, and he winced when he came to a stop in front of his destination, where half the front picket fence lay rotting on the weed-choked ground. Yes, there it was, number three-twenty—the old Granville house, the house he and Mary had thrown rocks at and made wishes on the night they'd found each other at the high school graduation dance. But this night, instead of the dark, ramshackle, forbidding haunted house, he saw an old house—still ramshackle—that was welcoming him with the warm glow of candlelight radiating into the rainy darkness from the shattered windows.

"Hey," a man hissed somewhere near the house, "these are the company's posters, and the company won't like this."

"How would you like to get a ticket next week?" another man answered—that was Bert the cop. "Haven't you got any romance in you?"

"Sure I have," the man snapped, "but I got rid of it!"

Bert struggled to unroll some posters, then snorted when he saw the picture. "Liver pills!" he exclaimed. "Who wants to see liver pills on their honeymoon? What they want is romantic places, beautiful places . . . places George wants to go!"

Whee-wheeet! A warning whistle! Ernie pushed aside a poster covering one of the windows and stuck his head out. "Hey, Bert!" he hollered. "Here he comes!"

"Come on, we got to get this up," Bert urged the other man. "He's coming."

"Who?"

"The groom, idiot! This is their honeymoon. Come on. Get that ladder."

The man glanced at the rain, the puddles, the leaky house. "What are they, ducks?"

"Just get that ladder up here."

"All right, all right."

"Hurry up!"

"I'm hurrying!"

On the porch, they finished covering a broken window with a travel poster facing inward just as George was dubiously making his way up the front walk—what was left of it.

Through the sound of the pouring rain George heard soft, romantic music, and as he climbed the creaking wooden steps to the porch he could see some kind of small hand-lettered sign on a crossbar in the curtained window of the front door. He peered closely in the dim light and read the sign: BRIDAL SUITE.

Suddenly the checkered curtain was whisked aside, and Ernie grinned through the opening that had once held glass. "Hiya—uh, ahem, good evening, sir." With all the flourish of a doorman at a posh hotel, he doffed his top hat and swept open the door. "*Entrez, monsieur, entrez.*" He held out his hand, as if for a tip.

George paused, stared at him a moment, and dipped his head. Water streamed from his hat brim into Ernie's outstretched palm. Ernie grimaced and closed the door.

George entered the house and stared. He shook his head in disbelief. Water was leaking through the ceiling, running down the peeling, faded wallpaper, dripping onto the broken stairs that led to the second floor. The whole dilapidated place seemed held together by nothing more than spiderwebs.

But then George let the words of the music wash over him:

"Islands of Hawaii, where skies of blue are calling me. Where balmy air and golden moonlight caress the waving palms of Waikiki . . . "

George did a double take. Across the front hall to his right, he spotted a candlelit bedroom, its old iron bed made up with fresh linens, a nightgown laid out across the covers, his-and-hers slippers side by side on the floor. He gulped and turned toward the living room.

There stood Mary, in a beautiful dress, her wedding corsage pinned to her shoulder, smiling brightly, eyes filled with love. But when George didn't say anything, she clutched her hands in front of her, anxious for his reaction.

Ernie took George's hat and coat, and the groom, smiling a little now, took a few steps toward the parlor, dodging a leak on his way.

"What is this?" George said, his voice a whisper.

All around the room, advertising posters covered the peeling wallpaper, the cracked plaster, the gaping windows—images of Florida, the South Seas, Hawaii, all magical in the flickering firelight.

On the table in front of Mary lay a wedding supper. The table was set with fine china, crystal, and candles on a checkered tablecloth, with a vase of fresh flowers gracing the center. Beyond that stood a bucket of iced champagne. To Mary's left, the Victrola spun its music, its revolving spindle hooked up to a belt that in turn cranked a spit holding Cornish game hens roasting over the crackling fire.

"Welcome home, Mr. Bailey," Mary said softly, lovingly.

George put his hands on his hips, flabbergasted, and whispered, "Well, I'll be . . . "

Impatient with his friend's slow reactions, Ernie sneaked up behind him and gave him a playful push into the room. Mission completed, Ernie then disappeared discreetly out the front door.

George went to his wife and folded her in his arms, still shaking his head in amazement. "Mary, Mary, where did you—"

She silenced him with a long kiss.

The Hawaiian crooning came to a scratchy end on the Victrola, and the next moment voices floated in through the windows—Bert and Ernie, harmonizing in the pouring rain: "I love you truly, truly, dear. Life with its sorrows, life with its tears . . . "

"Remember the night we broke the windows in this old house?" Mary whispered, her arms wrapped around her husband's neck. George nodded. "This is what I wished for."

"Darling," George whispered, "you're wonderful."

Outside in the pouring rain, Bert and Ernie grinned at the embracing silhouettes in the window and turned to each other as they drew out their final, harmonized "tru-ly deeeear." Time to leave the honeymooners to their paradise.

In the spirit of the moment, Ernie reached up, moved Bert's hat back an inch, and kissed him playfully on the forehead.

Not amused, Bert bonked the cabby on the head, squashing his top hat, and stomped off toward home.

9

In Potter's Field, where the unpainted wood-frame houses were hardly better than frontier shacks, men, women, and children were loading a truck with the Martini family's furniture and household items.

"Martini, you rented a new house?" old man Schultz stopped to inquire.

"Rent!" Martini exclaimed indignantly. "You hear what he say, Mr. Bailey?"

George was there with Mary, lending a hand with the Martinis' move. "What?"

Martini puffed his chest proudly. "I own the house. Me, Giuseppe Martini, I own my own house. No more we live like pigs in this Potter's Field." Martini waved to his wife. "Hurry, Marie!"

"Come on," George said. "Bring the baby."

The Martinis climbed aboard the truck piled high with all their possessions

"Like a king," Mrs. Martini remarked, awed by her family's sudden rise to the middle class.

"I'll take the kids in the car," George offered. There was really no other way.

"Oh, thank you, Mr. Bailey," Martini said.

"All right, kids . . . here, get in here," George called, holding open the door. They piled in—big kids, little kids, even the kid goat.

"Good-bye, everybody!" Martini shouted to the crowd of neighbors gathered to see them off.

George and Mary followed the Martini truck across town into a driveway in Bailey Park, a subdivision of small brick homes lined up on clean, paved roads—one of the few dreams that George had been able to turn into reality.

They stopped the car, and the kids got out. Mr. and Mrs. Martini were waiting on the front steps of the brand-new house.

"Mr. and Mrs. Martini, welcome home," George said grandly. The Martinis applauded, joined by a small crowd of well-wishers assembled on the lawn in front of the neat brick house.

"That old George, he's always making a speech," said a well-dressed man looking on from the street. He cupped his hands around his mouth and called out, "Hee-haw!"

George spotted him. "That's Wainwright," he remarked.

Mary looked over at the elegantly turned-out man standing in front of the gleaming black chauffeur-driven car and at the pretty, fur-draped wife sitting in the backseat. "Oh, who cares?" she said. She turned away to present Mrs. Martini with the traditional gifts to celebrate a new home: "Bread, that this house may never know hunger. Salt, that life may always have flavor."

George had something, too. "And wine, that joy and prosperity may reign forever." He handed the bottle to Martini. "Enter the Martini castle."

Potter's rent collector, a thin, energetic, bespectacled man named Reineman, laid a stack of maps on his boss's ornate desk. "Look, Mr. Potter," he said, "it's no skin off my nose. I'm just your little rent collector. But you can't laugh off this Bailey Park anymore. Look at it."

He jabbed a finger at the map just as the intercom buzzed.

The secretary's voice announced, "Congressman Black is here to see you."

"Oh, tell the congressman to wait," Potter shouted. His rent collector came first. "Go on."

"Fifteen years ago, a half dozen houses stuck here and there." Reineman jabbed at the map. "There's the old cemetery—squirrels, buttercups, daisies. I used to hunt rabbits there myself." He turned the sheet over to display the next map.

"Look at it today. Dozens of the prettiest little homes you ever saw. Ninety percent owned by suckers who used to pay rent to you! Your Potter's Field, my dear Mr. Employer, is becoming just that. And are the local yokels making with those David and Goliath wisecracks!"

"Oh, they are, are they?" Idiots, Potter thought. "Even though they know the Baileys haven't made a dime out of it," he said scornfully.

Reineman shared Potter's contempt for the unprofitable. "And you know very well why. The Baileys were all chumps. Every one of these homes is worth twice what it cost the building and loan to build. If I were you, Mr. Potter—"

"Well, you are not me," Potter cut him off.

Reineman repeated a pet phrase. "It's no skin off my nose." He rolled the maps, tucked them under his arm, and headed for the door, then stopped to get in a last word. "But one of these days, this bright young man is going to be asking George Bailey for a job."

The door closed behind Reineman. Potter frowned. "The Bailey family has been a boil on my neck long enough." He pressed the intercom button.

"Yes, sir?" his secretary answered.

"Come in here."

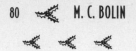

At Bailey Park, the Martinis were unloading their belongings while George and Mary chatted with Sam and Jane alongside the Wainwright limousine.

Sam was in his usual high spirits. "We just stopped in town to take a look at the new factory, and then we're going to drive on down to Florida."

"Oh . . . ," Mary breathed.

Lucky Sam, George was thinking.

Jane had a wonderful idea. "Why don't you have your friends join us?" she asked Sam.

"Why, sure!" he said. "Hey, why don't you kids drive down with us?"

"Oh, I'm afraid I couldn't get away, Sam," George cut in quickly.

"Still got the nose to the old grindstone, eh?" Sam kidded. "Jane, I offered to let George in on the ground floor in plastics, and he turned me down cold."

"Oh, now, don't rub it in." George smiled.

"I'm not rubbing it in," Sam assured him. "Well, I guess we better run along."

"Awfully happy to have met you, Mary," Jane said.

"Nice meeting you," Mary replied.

"So long, George. See you in the funny papers," Sam quipped as the gleaming car started off.

"Thanks for dropping around," George called.

"Florida!" Sam cheered. "Hee-haw!"

George walked back to his own old car and gave the door handle a pull. The door was stuck again, wouldn't you know it! *Slam!* He kicked it, hard.

10

George rolled the cigar in his mouth appreciatively and accepted a light from his host. "Thank you, sir," he said. "Quite a cigar, Mr. Potter."

"You like it? I'll send you a box," Potter offered.

Comfortable chair, fine cigar—George just wanted Potter to get to the point. "Well," he said, "I suppose I'll find out sooner or later, but just exactly what did you want to see me about?"

"George, now that's just what I like so much about you." Potter smiled. Any other businessman in Bedford Falls would be falling all over himself in Potter's presence. But not George Bailey.

"George, I'm an old man, and most people hate me," Potter stated matter-of-factly. "But I don't like them, either, so that makes it all even. You know just as well as I do that I run practically everything in this town but the Bailey Building and Loan. You know also that for a number of years I've been trying to get control of it or kill it. But I haven't been able to do it. You have been stopping me. In fact, you have beaten me, George, and as anyone in this county can tell you, that takes some doing. Take during the Depression, for instance. You and I were the only ones who kept our heads. You saved the building and loan, and I saved all the rest."

"Yes, well, most people say you stole all the rest," George commented.

"The envious ones say that, George, the suckers. Now, I have stated my side very frankly. Now let's look at your side. Young man, twenty-seven, twenty-eight, married, making say, forty a week."

"Forty-five."

"Forty-five. Forty-five. Out of which, after supporting your mother and paying your bills, you're able to keep, say, ten, if you skimp. A child or two comes along, and you won't even be able to save the ten. Now, if this young man of twenty-eight was a common, ordinary yokel, I'd say he was doing fine.

"But George Bailey is not a common, ordinary yokel. He's an intelligent, smart, ambitious young man who hates his job, who hates the building and loan almost as much as I do.

"A young man who's been dying to get out on his own ever since he was born. A young man—the smartest one of the crowd, mind you—a young man who has to sit by and watch his friends go places, because he's trapped. Yes, sir, trapped into frittering his life away playing nursemaid to a lot of garlic-eaters." Potter's meanness and bigotry played well in the false sanctity of his imposing office. He paused to measure George's reaction.

"Do I paint a correct picture, or do I exaggerate?" he insisted.

George didn't bite. "Now, what's your point, Mr. Potter?"

"My point? My point is, I want to hire you."

"Hire me?"

"I want you to manage my affairs, run my properties. George, I'll start you out at twenty thousand dollars a year."

George dropped his cigar. "Twenty thou—twenty thousand dollars a year?"

"You wouldn't mind living in the nicest house in town, buying your wife a lot of fine clothes, a couple of business trips to

New York a year, maybe once in a while to Europe. You wouldn't mind that, would you, George?"

"Would I?" He looked around. "You're not talking to somebody else around here, are you? You know, this is me. You remember me? George Bailey."

"Oh, yes, George Bailey. Whose ship has just come in—providing he has enough brains to climb aboard."

George smiled incredulously and regarded the fine cigar in his hand. He could see how men got addicted to cigars like this.

George wondered if Potter's deal might have a catch to it. "Well, how about the building and loan?"

"Oh, confound it, man," Potter scoffed, "are you afraid of success? I'm offering you a three-year contract at twenty thousand dollars a year, starting today. Is it a deal or isn't it?"

Potter's sudden impatience took George by surprise. "Well, Mr. Potter, I . . . I know I ought to jump at the chance, but I . . . I just wonder if it would be possible for you to give me twenty-four hours to think it over."

"Sure, sure, sure," Potter agreed, "you go on home and talk about it to your wife."

"I'd like to do that," George said.

"In the meantime, I'll draw up the papers."

"All right, sir."

Potter studied him. "Okay, George?"

"Okay, Mr. Potter."

The two men shook hands, and George looked long and hard into the old man's eyes. His smile faded as he thought of his father; he suddenly understood in his heart that he'd somehow fallen. He felt ashamed. He looked at the hand that had shaken Potter's, and he wiped it on his coat.

"No, no, no, no, now wait a minute here. I don't need twenty-four hours. I don't have to talk to anybody. I know right now, and the answer is no! No, doggone it!

"You sit around here, and you spin your little webs, and you think the whole world revolves around you and your money. Well, it doesn't, Mr. Potter. In the . . . in the whole vast configuration of things, I'd say you were nothing but a scurvy little spider. You"—he glared at the bodyguard—"and that goes for you, too." And to the people in the outer office: "And it goes for you, too!"

The house was mostly dark by the time George got home that night and trudged upstairs. Only the hall light was still burning, and he flicked that off as he silently eased open the bedroom door. Mary lay there in bed, already asleep, looking like an angel. And she is, George thought, she is.

He tiptoed into the room, pulling off his hat, his mind echoing with Potter's words: "You wouldn't mind living in the nicest house in town, buying your wife a lot of fine clothes, a couple of business trips to New York a year, maybe once in a while to Europe. . . ."

Other words flooded back to him, his own words, brash declarations he'd made to Mary on a moonlit night that seemed to have been centuries earlier: "I know what I'm going to do tomorrow and the next day and next year and the year after that . . . I'm shaking the dust of this crummy little town off my feet and I'm going to see the world. . . ."

George tossed his hat onto the chair and shrugged out of his suit coat as he walked over to their secondhand dresser and stared at his face in the mirror and remembered: "And then I'm going to build things. I'm going to build airfields, I'm going to build skyscrapers a hundred stories high, I'm going to build a bridge a mile long. . . ."

His eyes fell on that old goofy picture Mary had made for him—"George Lassos the Moon"—now framed like some kind of priceless masterpiece and hung on the wall.

"What is it you want, Mary?" he had said. "Do you want the moon? Just say the word, and I'll throw a lasso around it and pull it down. . . ."

George rested his palms on the dresser top; his shoulders sagged. All the plans he'd had, all the promises he'd made to himself and to Mary—things he'd never have, never see. His dreams shimmered before his eyes like moonlight, just as impossible to touch.

He could still taste Potter's offer, an overflowing goblet offered to a man dying of thirst.

And then he heard Mary, her fresh young voice singing saucily, a million nights ago, after they'd danced and fallen in the pool and wandered home together beneath the moonlight, two foolish young kids:

"Buffalo gals, won't you come out tonight, won't you come out tonight, won't you come out tonight . . ." Her voice was as sweet and real as if it were—

George spun around and stared at his wife. She seemed not to have moved, but as he went to the bed he could swear it really was Mary singing now, not just a memory in his head from that long-ago time.

"Buffalo gals, won't you come out tonight, a-a-a-and—"

George lay down on the bed and turned his wife over. Wide awake, she grinned impishly at him in the moonlight.

"Hi," he whispered.

"Hi."

He kissed her gently, his heart full. Oh, the things he could give this darling wife of his if he'd accepted Potter's offer.

"Mary Hatch," he whispered, caressing her hair. Then he sighed. "Why in the world did you ever marry a guy like me?"

"To keep from being an old maid," Mary quipped cheerfully.

George shook his head, too depressed to laugh. "You could have married Sam Wainwright or anybody else in town."

"Well, I didn't want to marry anybody else in town," Mary insisted. "I want my baby to look like you."

"We didn't even have a honeymoon," George went on, staring at their entwined hands. "I promised you—" His head snapped up. "Your what?"

Mary grinned. "My baby."

George sat bolt upright, and Mary sat up with him, beaming.

"You—you—you—your b—! Mary, you on the nest?"

"George Bailey lassoes stork," Mary announced.

"Lassoes the stork! Y-you mean you're—what is it, a boy or a girl?"

Mary nodded. "Mmm-hmmm!"

11

"Well," Joseph said to his trainee angel, "you've probably already guessed that George never leaves Bedford Falls."

"No!" Clarence exclaimed sadly.

Joseph nodded. Then he showed Clarence George Bailey's life over the next few years, but quickly now, like snippets in a newsreel at a moving picture show.

"Mary had her baby—a boy. Then she had another one—a girl. Day after day she worked away, remaking the old Granville house into a home."

Clarence could see Mary sewing curtains and covering the spotted old walls with bright new wallpaper.

"Night after night George came back late from the office. Potter was bearing down hard."

Clarence saw an image of George arriving home looking tired and discouraged. When he grabbed the railing to climb the stairs, the knob on the newel post came off in his hand, and he frowned at it, as if that one rounded wooden knob in need of repair epitomized his entire life. Sighing, he jiggled it back into place, to be fixed another day.

"Then came a war," Joseph went on. "Ma Bailey and Mrs. Hatch joined the Red Cross and sewed. Mary had two more babies but still found time to run the USO.

"Sam Wainwright made a fortune in plastic hoods for planes, Potter became head of the draft board, Gower and Uncle Billy sold war bonds.

"Bert the cop was wounded in North Africa, got the Silver Star. Ernie the taxi driver parachuted into France. Marty helped capture the Remagen Bridge.

"And Harry—Harry Bailey topped them all. A Navy flier, he shot down fifteen planes, two of them as they were about to crash into a transport full of soldiers."

"Yes," Clarence said, trying to be patient, "but George . . . "

"George? Four-F on account of his ear. George fought the battle of Bedford Falls—air raid warden, paper drives, scrap drives, rubber drives. Like everybody else, on V-E Day he wept and prayed. On V-J Day he wept and prayed again."

"Joseph," Franklin interrupted, "now show him what happened today."

"Yes, sir."

Clarence watched closely, eagerly, for he knew what he was about to see would be central to his mission, a mission he hoped would at long last earn him his wings. Besides, he was growing quite fond of this George Bailey, and he was worried about him.

"This morning," Joseph began, "day before Christmas, about ten A.M. Bedford Falls time . . . "

George Bailey was strolling downtown in his hat and overcoat, scarf wrapped around his neck, pipe clenched between his teeth, a Christmas wreath looped over one arm and a hefty stack of newspapers under the other. People were out and about with last-minute Christmas chores, and traffic was moving steadily despite several inches of snow on the ground.

"Hey, Ernie," George called out as he came alongside his friend, who stood talking on a public telephone next to his parked cab. "Look at that!" Bursting with pride, he held out a copy of the morning newspaper so Ernie could read the front-page headlines:

PRESIDENT DECORATES HARRY BAILEY

LOCAL BOY WINS CONGRESSIONAL MEDAL OF HONOR

CITY TO CELEBRATE HERO'S HOMECOMING

There was even a large photograph of the President pinning on the medal, and another of Harry in his uniform, smiling.

Ernie nodded. "Gonna snow again," he said, and turned back to his call.

"What do you mean, it's going to snow?" George howled, shaking the paper. "Look at the headlines!"

Ernie laughed and hung up. "I know, I know, George, and it's marvelous. Commander Harry Bailey!"

"Mr. Gower," George called out as his old boss approached, "look at this!" He passed out papers to both his friends, then hurried across the street.

Moments later he burst into the offices of the Bailey Brothers Building and Loan Association, holding up the papers like a newsboy and shouting, "Extra! Extra! Read all about it!"

"George! George!" Eustace cried. "It's Harry now, on long distance from Washington. Hey, he reversed the charges. It's okay, isn't it?"

"Reversed the charges, of course it is—for a hero?" George threw the papers on the counter and grabbed the phone. Eustace leaned in close to hear, while Cousin Tilly listened in on her headset.

"Harry?" George bellowed. "Oh, you old seven kinds of a son of a gun. Congratulations! How's Mother standing it? . . . She did? What do you know!" He held the phone away and told the others, "Mother had lunch with the President's wife."

"Wait till Martha hears about this!" Tilly exclaimed.

"What did she have to eat?" Eustace wanted to know.

"What'd they have to eat—oh, Harry, you should see what they're cooking up in the town for you! . . . Oh, they are?" He held the phone away again. "The Navy's going to fly Mother home this afternoon."

"In a plane?"

George gave Eustace a pained look. "What, Harry? Uncle Billy?" He turned to Tilly. "Has Uncle Billy come in yet?"

Tilly shook her head. "He stopped at the bank first."

"He's not here right now, Harry. But look . . . "

Eustace started to walk away, then jumped. In the excitement, he'd forgotten about the stern-looking little man in thick glasses sitting stiffly in the chair just outside George's office, drumming his fingertips impatiently on a leather briefcase almost as large as he was.

"George," Eustace whispered, poking his boss in the back.

"Now, Harry," George said, sitting on the edge of Tilly's desk, "tell me all about it—"

"George," Eustace whispered again, more insistently, "that man is here again."

"What man?"

"B-B-B-Bank examiner."

"Oh." George glanced over at the man, then quickly stood up. "Harry, talk to Eustace for a minute, will you? I'll be right back." He tossed the Christmas wreath on Tilly's desk, straightened his tie, adjusted his expression, and walked over to shake the man's hand. "Good morning, sir."

The man stood and barked, "Carter—bank examiner."

"Mr. Carter, Merry Christmas."

"Merry Christmas," the man said automatically.

"We're all excited around here," George explained as he grabbed a newspaper from the counter and held it out for Carter to see. "My brother just got the Congressional Medal of Honor. The President just decorated him."

"Yeah, well, I guess they do those things," Carter mumbled, scanning the page. Then he looked back up at George, who stood a good head and a half taller. "Well, I trust you had a good year."

"Good year?" George paused, then tried to worm a smile out of the old stick-in-the-mud. "Ah, well, between you and me, Mr. Carter, we're broke."

The man didn't blink. "Yeah, very funny."

George cleared his throat. "Ahem, well . . . right in here, Mr. Carter . . . "

"Although I shouldn't wonder, when you okay reverse charges on personal long-distance calls," Carter admonished him.

"George," Tilly asked, "shall we hang up?"

"No, no. He wants to talk to Uncle Billy. You just hold on."

"Now, if you'll cooperate," Carter said gruffly, "I'd like to finish with you by tonight. I want to spend Christmas in Elmira with my family."

"I don't blame you at all, Mr. Carter," George said, leading the man into a private office. "Just step right in here. We'll fix you up."

What a sourpuss, George thought. And what a way to spend Christmas Eve!

12

Uncle Billy fairly danced down the snowy streets of Bedford Falls with his copy of the newspaper—all about his famous hero nephew—tucked under his arm.

As he passed the YOU ARE NOW IN BEDFORD FALLS sign he paused to watch the men across the street hanging red, white, and blue bunting on the town hall railing, along with a huge WELCOME HOME HARRY BAILEY sign.

"Hey, be sure you spell the name right!" Billy called out before dashing across the slushy road to the bank.

Inside, he hurried to a counter to fill out the deposit slip. "December twenty-fourth," he read aloud as he wrote. He opened a plain, rumpled white envelope and thumbed through the cash. "Eight thousand . . . "

A commotion at the bank entrance caught his attention. Several bank employees were bowing obsequiously and holding the door open, shouting, "Merry Christmas"—not to an ordinary customer, but to their boss, the eminent Mr. Henry F. Potter, being wheeled by his silent bodyguard toward his office.

The old tyrant was scowling at the morning newspaper he held in his hands. When Uncle Billy saw that, he couldn't help himself—he grabbed his envelope and hurried over. "Well, good morning, Mr. Potter! What's the news?" he gloated.

Grinning broadly, he snatched the paper from Potter and pretended to read the headlines for the first time. "Well, well, well. Harry Bailey wins Congressional Medal. That couldn't be one of the Bailey boys!" He shook his head. "You just can't keep those Baileys down, now can you, Mr. Potter?"

Potter had been glowering through Billy Bailey's entire spiel, and now the only retort he could think of was "How does Slacker George feel about that?"

"Very jealous, very jealous," Uncle Billy teased. "He only lost three buttons off his vest. Of course, Slacker George would have gotten two of these medals if he had gone."

"Bad ear," Potter muttered.

"Yes. But after all, Potter, some people like George had to stay at home. Not every heel," he said meaningfully, "was in Germany and Japan." He folded the newspaper and returned it to Potter.

Potter grabbed it and scowled, motioning for his bodyguard to wheel him into his office.

Chuckling gleefully, Uncle Billy scooped up his deposit slip and his own newspaper from the counter and bounced over to the teller's window.

"Good morning, Mr. Bailey," the teller said cheerfully.

Still cackling, Billy slid his passbook under the teller's bars. "Good morning, Horace."

The teller stamped his passbook, then looked up expectantly. "Uh, I guess you forgot something."

"Huh?"

"You forgot something."

"What?"

"Well, aren't you going to make a deposit?"

"Oh, sure—sure I am."

Horace chuckled. "Well, then, it's usually customary to bring the money with you."

"Oh, shucks." Grinning sheepishly, Billy reached into his

inside right coat pocket for the envelope with the eight thousand dollars. He frowned and began fumbling through his other pockets, inside and out, even the pockets of his trousers, more and more embarrassed as he noticed the growing line of people behind him watching with interest.

His pockets were empty. Nothing. No envelope. No money anywhere. "I know I had it."

The teller knew Billy's habits well and, pointing to a finger tied with string, kindly suggested, "What about that finger there?"

"Hmmm? Well, I . . . "

Potter was still scowling as he spread the morning paper out on his office desk. "Bailey!" he grumbled. Suddenly his eyes widened. A rumpled white envelope lay in the center of the paper. Potter snatched it up and opened it, astonished as he fanned through the thick stack of bills. Behind him, still in his hat and coat, his bulldog-faced bodyguard froze in the midst of undoing a button. He stared, but as always he uttered not a word.

Potter glanced up at the door, thinking hard. He stuffed the cash back into the envelope, folded the newspaper around it, and shouted excitedly at his bodyguard, "Take me back there. Hurry up!"

The man obeyed, but not before his frantically eager boss barked again, "Come on, look sharp!" and pounded impatiently on the armrest of his wheelchair.

But when Potter reached the door, he merely opened it a crack to peer out into the bank. He immediately spotted Billy Bailey frenziedly searching the customer counter, digging through the metal wastebasket, and scanning the bank as he rummaged through his pockets a final time before stumbling through the bank's revolving door to the street.

Potter knew, of course, what Bailey was looking for, but he didn't call after him. Instead, he eased the door closed and mumbled to his man, "Take me back." Silently, the bodyguard wheeled him to his desk. Potter rubbed his chin, deep in thought.

Back at the building and loan office, George had gotten the bank examiner settled in an office. "Just make yourself at home, Mr. Carter. I'll get those books for you."

But George had a visitor. Violet stood near his office, dressed in a shapely black suit and stylish fur hat, looking as though she had just stepped out of a fashion magazine.

"Oh, hello, Vi."

"George, can I see you for a second?" she asked softly, her usual wink and flirtatious smile completely absent.

"Why, of course you can. Come on in the office here."

Just then Billy raced in, clearly in a dither; no one really paid attention, since this was often his manner. Still clutching the passbook in his left hand, he held up his arm, and his pet crow flew to him, squawking as it dug its claws into the tweed of his jacket.

"Oh, Uncle Billy," George called just before he closed the door to his office, "talk to Harry. He's on the telephone."

"Hurry, Uncle Billy, hurry," Tilly urged. "Long distance, Washington. You know, your nephew? Remember? Harry?"

Distracted, Billy took the phone. "Hello, hello? . . . Yes, Harry, yes, everything . . . everything's fine." And he promptly hung up. "I should have my head examined," he muttered. "Eight thousand dollars. It's got to be here somewhere."

Tilly and Eustace looked puzzled as Billy wandered distractedly into his office.

Meanwhile, behind the closed doors of his own office,

George had just finished writing a character reference for Violet. He folded it and put it into an envelope. "Here you are."

"Character?" she muttered, tucking the envelope into her purse. "If I had any character, I'd—"

"Ah, well, it takes a lot of character to leave your hometown and start all over again." He stood up, digging into his pockets, then slipped some bills into Violet's hand.

"Oh, no, George, don't—"

"Here, now, you're broke, aren't you?"

"I know, but—"

"What do you want to do," he teased her, "hock your furs and that hat?"

Violet smiled a little.

"Want to walk to New York?" George went on. "You know, they charge for meals and rent up there. Just the same as they do in Bedford Falls."

"Yeah, sure . . . "

George walked her toward the door. "Ah, that's a loan, now. That's my business—building and loan. Besides, you'll get a job. Good luck to you."

Violet gazed up at him in adoration for a moment, then whispered earnestly, "I'm glad I know you, George Bailey." She kissed him, leaving a bold red smear across his cheek.

"Yeah, well . . . ," George mumbled, embarrassed. "Say hello to New York for me," he said as they left his office.

"Yeah, yeah, sure I will."

"Now, let's hear from you once in a while."

Violet pulled out a handkerchief and started rubbing the lipstick off his cheek. Eustace and Tilly glanced up, and their jaws dropped. Carter came out of his office to stare.

George shook her hand. "Merry Christmas, Vi."

"Merry Christmas, George," she replied with a tremor in her voice, then turned quickly and hurried from the office.

The bank examiner's loud sigh telegraphed his impatience and disapproval. "Mr. Bailey—"

"Oh, Mr. Carter, I'm sorry. I'll be right with you." He turned to Tilly and asked, "Uncle Billy in?"

"Yeah, he's in his office."

George opened Billy's door. "Uncle . . . what's going on?"

Billy Bailey was down on his hands and knees, scrambling beneath his desk, still wearing his hat and coat. His office looked as if he'd left the window open on a windy day; papers were scattered everywhere.

"The bank examiner's here," George told him.

Billy rose to his feet, looking like a frightened child, papers crumpled in his hands. "He's here?" he croaked.

"Well, yeah, he wants the accounts payable to—" George frowned. "What's the matter with you?"

Trembling, Billy waved George into the office and slammed the door.

Eustace and Tilly exchanged curious looks.

Moments later, George slammed out of Billy's office and dashed to the safe. He staggered back with a look of panic on his face, then flew to the cash drawer at the front counter and rifled through its contents. He stiffened when behind him he heard Carter come out of his office, felt the man's curious stare boring into his back. "Eustace?" said softly.

"Yeah?"

"Come here a minute." Eustace came up beside him. George asked quietly, "Did you see Uncle Billy with any cash last night?"

"He had it on his desk, counting it before he closed up."

George didn't stop to put on his hat and overcoat. He ran out into the snowy streets with only his scarf flapping around the neck of his business suit. Billy scurried to keep up.

"Now, look," George asked him patiently as they walked, "did you buy anything?"

Billy shook his head adamantly. "Nothing. Not even a stick of gum."

"All right, all right. Now, we'll go over every step you took since you left the house."

"Right! This way."

Across the street, Henry F. Potter peeked through the blinds of his office at Billy Bailey leading George Bailey along a looping, zigzagging path through town, searching the ground as if they'd lost something.

Potter's expression didn't change as he let the blinds snap closed.

Hours later, after a fruitless search, George and his uncle sat in Billy's house.

Billy had collapsed at his desk, dazed, exhausted, confused, his desktop disheveled by their frenetic search.

". . . And did you put the envelope in your pocket?" George asked for the thousandth time, leaning across the desk.

"Yeah, maybe . . . maybe . . . "

"Maybe? Maybe? I don't want any maybe!" George shouted, roughly grabbing his uncle's lapels. "We've got to find that money!"

Billy moaned, "I'm no good to you, George. I can't—"

"Uncle Billy, look, do you realize what's going to happen to us if we don't find it?" George cried. He fought to control himself, desperately searching his mind for some new ideas. "Listen to me. Do you have any secret hiding place here in the house? Someplace you would have put it? Someplace you'd hide the money?"

"I've gone over the whole house, even the rooms that have been locked since I lost Laura." Uncle Billy dissolved into sobs.

"Listen to me, listen to me!" George said, growing more and more frantic. "Think—think!"

"I can't think anymore, George. I can't think anymore—it hurts!"

Out of control now, George grabbed his uncle by the lapels again and yanked him to his feet, screaming, "Where's the money, you silly, stupid old fool? Where's that money? Do you realize what this means? It means bankruptcy and scandal—and prison!" He flung the terrified man back into the chair. "That's what it means. One of us is going to jail! Well, it's not going to be me!" Gasping, he turned to leave, hauling off and kicking a box of junk before he staggered out of the room.

Uncle Billy buried his face in his arms and sobbed, oblivious to the pet squirrel that had scampered onto his shoulder.

13

Janie Bailey was playing the piano, struggling to get the chords of "Hark the Herald Angels Sing" right, as George entered his house at 320 Sycamore. He slammed the door and stood in the front hall, brushing snow from his suit jacket.

"Hello, darling," Mary called out brightly.

"Hello, Daddy," the children—Pete, Janie, and Tommy—chimed in.

Mary, dressed in a slim black dress with a white crocheted collar and wearing a strand of pearls, stood on a step stool trimming the Christmas tree. Sparkling garlands dappled with ornaments crisscrossed the room, and a banner proclaimed MERRY CHRISTMAS in foot-tall glittery letters.

Mary glanced at the tree. "How do you like it?"

George sneezed.

"Bless you!" everyone said at once.

Mary and the two boys hurried over to greet him. "Did you bring the wreath?" Mary asked.

"Yeah, Daddy, did you bring the wreath?" Pete repeated, a red and white Santa Claus hat on his head.

George drew a handkerchief from his pocket and blew his nose. "What wreath?"

"Well, the Merry Christmas wreath, for the window," Mary said.

"No, I left it at the office."

"Is it snowing?" she asked, brushing the wet flakes from his shoulder.

"Yeah, just started."

"Where's your coat and hat?"

"Left them at the office."

Mary's voice softened. "What's the matter?"

"Nothing's the matter. Everything's all right."

George sat down in a worn armchair and stared at the floor. Little Tommy ran over and growled at his father through his Santa Claus mask and beard.

Turning back to the tree, Mary handed Pete, their older boy, a huge star for the top. "Go ahead, Pete, you're a big boy. You can put the star up. Way up at the top. That's it." She passed him more tinsel. "Fill in that little bare spot right there. That's it."

Janie was still banging away at the piano, Tommy was still growling at his father's knee, and suddenly George grabbed the little boy and hugged him tightly with trembling arms, crying softly, surrendering to his fears.

"Isn't it wonderful about Harry?" Mary chattered on, oblivious, her face toward the tree. "We're famous, George. I'll bet I had fifty calls today about the parade, the banquet. Your mother's so excited, she—"

She turned and saw her husband's face, saw him kissing Tommy almost desperately. His hair was mussed, his tie askew, his unshaven face contorted—something was wrong, terribly wrong. Even after his toughest days at the office, Mary had never seen him look like this.

George recovered himself somewhat and sat biting his knuckles, thinking, thinking, his mind spinning. What on earth was he going to do? What was he going to do? And all the while Tommy sat on his lap, decorating his daddy's head with strands of tinsel, and Janie kept playing "Hark the Herald Angels Sing."

"Must she keep playing that?" George broke in.

"I have to practice it for the party tonight, Daddy," Janie insisted.

"Mom said we can stay up till midnight and sing Christmas carols!" Pete exclaimed.

"Can you sing, Daddy?" Tommy asked.

George frowned and wiped the tinsel from his head.

"Better hurry and shave," Mary suggested gently as Tommy hopped down. "The families will be here soon."

"Families!" George exploded from his chair. "I don't want the families over here."

Mary took her husband's hand and led him from the noisy living room. "Come on out in the kitchen with me while I finish dinner."

"'Scuse me!" Tommy was tagging along, yanking on his daddy's coat for attention. "'Scuse me!" But George didn't notice.

"Have a hectic day?" Mary asked.

"Oh, yeah, another big red-letter day for the Baileys," George said sarcastically.

"Daddy," Pete said, following his parents into the kitchen, "the Browns next door have a new car. You should see it."

"Well, what's the matter with our car?" George yelled. "Isn't it good enough for you?"

Pete took a step backward and replied meekly, "Yes, Daddy."

"'Scuse me," Tommy said again, yanking and yanking on his daddy's coattails. "'Scuse me!"

"Excuse you for what?" George snapped.

"I burped!"

Mary smiled as she tied the strings of her white apron. "All right, Tommy, you're excused. Now go upstairs and see if little Zuzu wants anything."

"Zuzu?" George asked. "Well, what's the matter with Zuzu?"

"Oh, she's just got a cold. She's in bed. Caught it coming home from school." Mary opened the oven and pulled out two trays of muffins and then the roasting pan. "They gave her a flower for a prize and she didn't want to crush it, so she didn't button up her coat."

"What is it, a sore throat or what?"

"Just a cold. The doctor says it's nothing serious."

"The doctor? Was the doctor here?"

"Yes, I called him right away. He says it's nothing to worry about."

"Is she running a temperature? What is it?"

"Just a teensy one. Ninety-nine six. She'll be all right."

"Gosh, it's this old house. I don't know why we don't all have pneumonia. This drafty old barn! Might as well be living in a refrigerator." George stuffed his hands in his pockets and paced the small kitchen. "Why did we have to live here in the first place and stay around this measly, crummy old town?"

"George, what's wrong?"

"Wrong? Everything's wrong! You call this a happy family? Why did we have to have all these kids?"

"Dad"—Pete came in with a pencil and tablet—"how do you spell *frankincense?*"

"I don't know. Ask your mother," George muttered, brushing past his son in the doorway.

"Where are you going?" Mary asked.

"Going up to see Zuzu."

"He told me to write a play for tomorrow," Pete said defensively.

George stomped up the stairs, gritting his teeth at the sound of Janie's persistent pounding on the piano, over and over, never stopping—and then the newel post knob came off in his hand.

Muttering an oath, he grabbed it like a baseball, wanting to smash it through the wall, but he caught himself and managed to be satisfied with simply bashing it back into place. He ran up the stairs to Zuzu's room and found her sitting up in bed, holding a flower and smiling brightly. "Hi, Daddy."

"Well, what happened to you?" George asked gently.

"I won a flower." She threw back her covers and started to get out of bed.

"Wait, now," he said. "Where do you think you're going?"

"I want to give my flower a drink."

George sat down on the edge of the bed and tucked her back under the covers. "All right, all right. Here, give Daddy the flower. I'll give it a drink."

As she handed him the flower several petals drifted to the blanket.

"Look, Daddy." She picked up the petals and looked up into George's eyes. "Paste it!"

George's voice was mellow now, calm, his own problems forgotten for a moment. "Yeah, all right, all right, give it here. Now, I'll paste this together." Turning slightly, he pretended to paste, but instead tucked the loose petals into the watch pocket of his trousers. He turned back to his daughter and held out the flower.

"There it is, good as new. Now we'll give the flower a drink." He slipped it into the water glass that sat on Zuzu's nightstand.

The little girl smiled.

"Now will you do something for me?" he asked softly.

"What?" she whispered.

"Will you try to get some sleep?" he whispered back.

"I'm not sleepy," she answered. "I want to look at my flower."

"I know, I know." He eased her back onto her pillow and continued whispering. "But you just go to sleep, and then you can dream about it, and it'll be a whole garden."

"It will?"

"Uh-huh."

Zuzu stared at her flower, content now.

George felt her forehead and frowned with worry, and abruptly, along with Zuzu's cold, all his problems flooded back into his mind.

Downstairs the telephone rang, and three children's voices sang out, "Telephone!"

"I'll get it," Mary said, hurrying to the front hallway. "Hello . . . Yes, this is Mrs. Bailey . . . Oh, thank you, Mrs. Welch. I'm sure she'll be all right. The doctor says that she ought to be out of bed in time to have her Christmas dinner."

"Is that Zuzu's teacher?" George demanded, coming down the stairs.

"Yes."

"Let me speak to her." He yanked the phone from Mary's hands. "Hello? Hello, Mrs. Welch? This is George Bailey. I'm Zuzu's father. Say, what kind of a teacher are you, anyway? What do you mean, sending her home like that, half naked? Do you realize she'll probably end up with pneumonia on account of you?"

"George!" Mary tried to stop him.

"Is this the sort of thing we pay taxes for—to have teachers like you? Silly, stupid, careless people who send our kids home without any clothes on? You know, maybe my kids aren't the best-dressed kids in town, maybe they don't have any decent clothes—"

Mary, horrified, finally managed to grab the telephone away.

George paced, muttering, "Aw, that stupid . . . "

"Hello, Mrs. Welch?" Mary said brightly. "I want to apologize . . . Hello? Hello?" She gave George a stern look. "She's hung up."

"Aw, I'll hang her up!"

Another voice came braying through the receiver. "Hey, you, I'll knock your block off—"

"What is that?" George grabbed the phone again. "Hello, who's this? . . . Oh, Mr. Welch . . . Okay, that's fine, Mr. Welch. Give me a chance to tell you what I really think of your wife."

"George—"

"Will you get out and let me handle this?" he yelled at Mary. "Hello? Hello? What? . . . Oh, you will, huh? Okay, Mr. Welch. Anytime you think you're man enough. Hello? Any— Arrgghh!" He slammed the phone down and stomped into the living room. Pete, in his Santa Claus hat, was sitting at a table writing, Tommy was shoving at the rug with a carpet sweeper, and Janie was still banging out "Hark the Herald Angels Sing."

"Daddy, how do you spell *hallelujah?*" Pete asked.

"How should I know? What do you think I am, a dictionary? Tommy, stop that! Stop it! Janie, haven't you learned that silly tune yet? You've played it over and over again. Now stop it. Stop it!"

The music stopped abruptly. Mary and the children stared at George as he staggered to the front of the room, running his hands through his hair.

In the silence, only George's heavy breathing could be heard as he stared at his office setup in the corner of the room: drafting table covered with rolled-up plans, tables crowded with architectural models he'd built of skyscrapers and suspension bridges. This was his tiny corner, where he played at his dreams. George sneered at himself. Yes, that was where he played with stupid toys that meant nothing, that mocked his failures.

In a surge of rage, he kicked hard at the table and overturned it, destroying the suspension bridge; he smashed the models with his fist, shoved the plans from his drafting table, kicked and stomped his foolish projects as they tumbled to the floor.

His anger spent, he turned to face the silent, frightened stares of his wife and children. He took a few breaths, then said quietly, "I'm sorry, Mary, Janie, I'm sorry, I . . . I didn't mean that . . . you go on and practice."

Janie's lip trembled and her eyes filled with tears as she sat with her small hands on the keys. She didn't play.

"Pete, I owe you an apology, too," George went on softly. "I—I'm sorry. What do you want to know now?"

"Nothing, Daddy." Pete bit his lip.

For a moment no one moved. George stared at his family; they were gaping at him as if he were some stranger they'd never seen, some wild man who'd broken into their house and meant them harm.

"Well, what's the matter with everybody?" George snapped, his anger rising again. "Janie, go on. I told you to practice. Now go on, play!"

Janie burst into tears. "Oh, Daddy!"

Angry now herself, Mary took Tommy's hand and led him over to the piano so she could put an arm around Janie. "George," she admonished, gathering the children around her, "why must you torture the children? Why don't you—"

She didn't finish her sentence.

"Mary . . . ," George said, a whispered plea.

She had never looked at him that way before.

And suddenly he couldn't bear it—he had to get away. He staggered to the front door and fled into the snowy night.

After a moment of stunned silence, Mary went straight to the phone. "Bedford two-four-seven, please."

"Is Daddy in trouble?" Peter asked quietly as the children gathered around.

"Yes, Peter."

"Shall I pray for him?" Janie asked.

"Yes, Janie. Pray very hard."

"Me too?" little Tommy piped up.
"You too, Tommy."
The children ran to their rooms.
"Hello? Uncle Billy?"

14

The snow was coming down pretty hard by the time George found himself staggering toward the only place left in town where he might try to get help—the office of Henry F. Potter. He was surprised at how quickly Potter agreed to see him.

The last time he'd sat in this leather chair in Potter's office, he'd been smoking expensive cigars and discussing rich salaries and trips to Europe. He had been filled with dreams and ideals then.

Now he sat in the same chair, hatless, coatless, covered with snow, his clothes rumpled, an idealistic man brought to his knees. He'd come crawling. Begging.

"I'm in trouble, Mr. Potter," George said, his voice subdued and humble. "I need help. Through some sort of an accident, my company's short on their accounts. The bank examiner got there today, and I've got to raise eight thousand dollars immediately."

"Oh, so that's what the reporters wanted to talk to you about."

"The reporters?" George exclaimed.

"Yes, they called me up from your building and loan," Potter explained. "Oh, there's a man over there from the DA's office, too. He's looking for you."

George leaned forward across the desk. "Please help me, Mr. Potter. Help me, won't you please? Can't you see what it means to my family? I'll pay any sort of a bonus on the loan, any interest. If you still want the building and loan, why, I—"

"George," Potter interrupted, "could it possibly be there's a slight discrepancy in the books?"

"No, sir. There's nothing wrong with the books," George said desperately. "I've just misplaced eight thousand dollars— I can't find it anywhere!"

Potter stared at him, feigning surprise. "You misplaced eight thousand dollars?"

George lowered his head and muttered, "Yes, sir."

Potter glanced behind him at his bodyguard, the ever silent companion who had been with him earlier that day at the bank when he'd found the plain, rumpled white envelope filled with money in his morning newspaper, when he'd seen Billy Bailey frantically searching for lost cash in the bank lobby before dashing into the streets.

The bodyguard didn't even blink.

Potter turned back to George. "Have you notified the police?"

"No, sir. I didn't want the publicity. Harry's homecoming tomorrow—"

Potter cackled. "They're going to believe that one," he said sarcastically. "What've you been doing, George? Playing the market with the company's money?"

"No, sir, no, sir. I haven't."

"What is it—a woman, then? You know, it's all over town that you've been giving money to Violet Bick."

"What?" George gasped.

"Not that it makes any difference to me, but why did you come to me? Why don't you go to Sam Wainwright and ask him for the money?"

"I can't get hold of him. He's in Europe."

"Well, what about all your other friends?"

"They don't have that kind of money, Mr. Potter. You know that. You're the only one in town that can help me."

"I see. I've suddenly become quite important." He chuckled, thoroughly enjoying this, watching George Bailey squirm. Potter cleared his throat and, knowing the answer before he spoke, asked coolly, "What kind of security would I have, George? You got any stocks?"

"No, sir."

"Bonds? Real estate? Collateral of any kind?"

George reached into his inside coat pocket and pulled out some folded papers. "I have some life insurance, a fifteen-thousand-dollar policy."

"Yes . . . how much is your equity in it?"

George looked down. "Five hundred dollars."

"Five hundred dollars!" Potter exclaimed. "And you ask me to lend you eight thousand?" Potter removed his glasses and glared at George, his voice infused with years of pent-up hatred. "Look at you. You used to be so cocky! You were going to go out and conquer the world. You once called me a warped, frustrated old man. What are you but a warped, frustrated young man? A miserable little clerk crawling in here on your hands and knees and begging for help. No securities, no stocks, no bonds, nothing but a miserable little five-hundred-dollar equity in a life insurance policy."

Humiliated, George stared down at the insurance papers clutched in his trembling hands.

Potter put his glasses back on and cackled gleefully. "Why, you're worth more dead than alive!"

George's head shot up, his anguish reflected in his eyes as he stared helplessly at the man.

"Why don't you go to the riffraff you love so much and ask them to let you have eight thousand dollars?" Potter taunted, rubbing his hands together. "You know why? Because they'd run you out of town on a rail. But I tell you what I'm going to do for you, George. . . ."

Potter reached for his phone, and for a moment there was a tiny light of hope in George's eyes.

"Since the state examiner is still here," Potter went on as he dialed, "as a stockholder of the building and loan, I'm going to swear out a warrant for your arrest. Misappropriation of funds, manipulation, malfeasance . . . "

Stunned, George stuffed the policy back into his pocket as he slowly rose to his feet and headed for the door.

"All right, George, go ahead," Potter called after him, laughing. "You can't hide in a little town like this. . . . Yeah, Bill?" he said into the phone. "This is Potter. . . ."

George crossed the street to his car, oblivious to the falling snow, the strings of colored Christmas lights, the people passing by—not knowing where he was going, driven only by his despair. As if to mock his desolation, his car door wouldn't open. He yanked on it hard, again and again, and finally stepped on the running board and climbed through the window into the front seat.

Before he knew it, he found himself hanging on to the wooden bar at Martini's, trying to dull the pain with shot glasses of liquor.

Martini's resounded with cheerful Italian songs and the chatter of happy customers.

"Ah, Merry Christmas!" Martini exclaimed, ushering some customers to a table. "Glad you came."

"How about some of that good spaghetti?" a man asked.

"We got everything!"

George, his mind in turmoil, was unaware of the activities around him. As his head sank deep between his shoulders he noticed the insurance policy sticking out of his coat. He fingered it thoughtfully a moment before a look of horror and revulsion twisted his face, and he pushed it back down into his pocket.

Rubbing his mouth, he whispered behind his trembling fist, "Oh, God . . . Oh, God . . ." And then he was gripping both hands, his forearms propped against the wooden bar, half drunk and praying as he'd never done before: "Dear Father in heaven," he muttered into his hands, "I'm not a praying man. But if you're up there and you can hear me . . . show me the way. I'm at the end of my rope. I . . . show me the way, God."

Nick the bartender leaned over the counter and spoke gently to his friend. "Are you all right, George? Want someone to take you home?"

George, sweat breaking out on his brow, shrugged.

Mr. Martini came up beside him and slipped an affectionate arm around his shoulders. "Why you drink so much, my friend? Please go home, Mr. Bailey. This is Christmas Eve."

The man sitting one stool down at the bar turned, his drink halfway to his mouth. "Bailey? Which Bailey?"

"This is Mr. George Bailey," Nick said.

At that the man jumped up from his seat, pulled George to his feet, and punched him in the face, sending him sprawling across the floor. Women screamed and customers crowded around to see what was going on.

"And the next time you talk to my wife like that, you'll get worse!" the man shouted. "She cried for an hour. It isn't enough she slaves teaching your stupid kids how to read and write. You had to bawl her out—"

"You get out of here, Mr. Welch!" Martini shouted.

"Now, wait, I want to pay for my drink!"

"Never mind the money. You get out of here quick. You hit my best friend," Martini yelled as Nick hustled him out the door. "You get out!"

Nick and Martini hurried over to George and helped him up from the floor. "You all right, George?" Nick asked.

George was dazed, and his lip was bleeding, but he managed to mutter, "Who was that?"

"He gone. No worry," Martini assured him. "His name is Welch. He no come into my place no more."

"Oh—Welch." The teacher's husband. "That's what I get for praying," he muttered.

"The last time he come in here. You hear that, Nick?"

"Yeah, you bet."

George felt his pockets. "Where's my insurance policy?" He pulled it out and headed for the door.

"Oh, no, please. Don't go out this way, Mr. Bailey," Martini pleaded, pulling on George's arm. "No, no, you no feel good. Please, sit down and rest."

"I'm all right," George hollered. He shook the little man off and headed out the door.

Soon George was in his car, driving, swerving recklessly along the slippery streets, heading he didn't know where, just driving, driving through the heavy snowfall until—*crunch!*

George smashed the car into a huge tree.

He flung open the door and tumbled out into the night. The car door that often stuck now wouldn't close, and he slammed it, slammed it again, then kicked it violently.

The owner of the property hurried out of his large home and ran down the front walk under an umbrella. "What do you think you're doing?" He ran his hand over the deep gash in the tree trunk. "Now look what you did!" he shouted at George. "My great-grandfather planted this tree!"

George waved him away as he wandered off into the snow.

"Hey, you—hey, you!" the man shouted. "Come back here, you drunken fool! Get this car out of here!"

George kept walking till the hiss of the falling snow muffled the man's angry voice in the distance.

Honk! Honk!

George froze, caught in the headlights of a delivery truck that had barely managed to screech to a halt and avoid running him down. "Hey, what's the matter with you?" the driver hollered. "Look where you're going!"

George staggered backward as the truck passed, then he followed its route to the nearby bridge, trudging unsteadily onto the pedestrian walkway, his hand knocking snow from the handrail as he used it to steady himself.

Nearly halfway across, George's steps slowed; he seemed to lose his way or his reason for going on. With both hands on the railing, he stared down into the churning waters of the river below.

A few steps away, a plump, white-haired old man wearing a hat and overcoat and polka-dot bow tie watched George closely with a half smile on his face, waiting to see what he would do.

But George didn't or couldn't—see him. Eyes wild, he looked to the left, to the right, making sure that no one was around, that no one would see him. Misery welled up in him; the dark waters below seemed to call to him, promising an answer, an end to his problems, an end to his pain.

George started to climb the railing.

But before he could climb over, someone else fell from the bridge and plunged feet first into the river.

"Help! . . . Help! Help!"

Startled out of his thoughts, George couldn't believe his eyes. He'd been so sure he was alone on the bridge, and now somebody—a man, it sounded like—was struggling in the water, screaming for help.

Forgetting his problems, George yanked off his coat, tossed it over the railing, and dived into the water to rescue the drowning man.

15

George plunged into the icy water, the long drop from the bridge forcing him deep below the surface. He struggled and kicked upward against the drag of the current, finally breaking the surface a few feet from the man bobbing in the waves.

George hooked his arm around the victim from behind and swam toward the shore. The man was older, heavyset—George was surprised at how easily he floated in his thick wool coat. Somehow he'd managed to keep his hat on, too.

The man's cries had brought the gatekeeper out from the little house at the end of the span; he lighted their way from above with the beam from his powerful flashlight. At last the water-soaked men made their way to the bank and into the refuge of the gatehouse.

Inside, a wood-burning stove radiated heat, warming the men and drying the sodden clothes draped around the tiny room on makeshift clotheslines. The gatekeeper, as was his custom, sat near the door chewing tobacco, his wooden chair propped against the wall, tipped on its back legs. George was seated near the stove in his long johns, wrapped up in a blanket, huddled miserably over a steaming mug. The would-be drowning victim stood a few feet away, looking little the worse for the ordeal, mildly attending to the frilly nightshirt he'd worn beneath his street clothes. The gatekeeper, a practical man, eyed the old man's outfit with raised eyebrows.

"I didn't have time to get some stylish underwear," the man explained. "My wife gave me this on my last birthday."

The gatekeeper pivoted his chair forward to use the spittoon.

"I passed away in it," the man mentioned.

The gatekeeper took his eyes off the target and fixed them on the man in the nightshirt. His chair legs slammed to the floor; he resumed chewing.

The old gent retrieved a book from his wet clothing and shook the water off it—*The Adventures of Tom Sawyer*. "You should read the new book Mark Twain is writing now," he said.

The keeper made an effort to bring the conversation closer to earth. "How'd you happen to fall in?" he asked.

"Oh, I didn't fall in," the little man explained. "I jumped in to save George."

George looked up. "You what? To save me?"

"Well, I did, didn't I?" the man asked. "You didn't go through with it, did you?"

"Go through with what?" George protested.

"Suicide," the man said brightly.

"It's against the law to commit suicide around here," the keeper noted.

"It's against the law where I come from, too," the little man agreed.

"Where do you come from?" the keeper asked, pivoting forward to use the spittoon again.

"Heaven," the little man said.

The keeper was puckered for the spit, but once again he found his eyes drawn off the mark to stare at the strange man in the nightshirt.

"I had to act quickly," the little old man went on to George. "That's why I jumped in. I knew if I were drowning, you'd try to save me. And you see, you did, and that's how I saved you."

"Very funny," George said sarcastically.

"Your lip's bleeding, George."

"Yeah, I got a bust in the jaw in answer to a prayer a little bit ago," George griped.

"Oh, no, no, George. I'm the answer to your prayer. That's why I was sent down here."

"How do you know my name?" George asked irritably.

"Oh, I know all about you. I've watched you grow up from a little boy."

George frowned. "What are you, a mind reader or something?"

"Oh, no," the little man chuckled.

"Well, what are you, then?"

"Clarence Odbody, AS two." Military delivery, like giving his name, rank, and serial number.

"AS two," George muttered. "What's that AS two?"

"Angel second class."

The gatekeeper's chair slid out from under him, and he crashed to the floor. If it hurt, he didn't notice—he got up very cautiously and reached for the door, gaping at Clarence. Careful not to make any sudden moves, he backed out, closed the door softly, and abandoned the station, dashing off into the snowy night.

Clarence didn't try to stop him. "Cheerio, my good man."

George rubbed his head. "Oh, brother. I wonder what Martini put in those drinks," he mumbled. He glanced at the kook he'd fished from the river. "Hey, what's with you?" he said. "What did you say just a minute ago? Why'd you want to save me?"

"That's what I was sent down for. I'm your guardian angel."

George figured he should have known he'd never get a straight answer from this guy. "I wouldn't be a bit surprised," George muttered.

"Ridiculous of you to think of killing yourself for money . . . eight thousand dollars." Clarence shook his head.

"Yeah, things like that—now, how'd you know that?" It didn't make any sense to George.

"I told you. I'm your guardian angel. I know everything about you."

George looked him over. Clarence was old. Kind of dumpy. Wearing some kind of lacy nightgown. "Well, you look about like the kind of an angel I'd get. Sort of a fallen angel, aren't you?" George looked over Clarence's shoulders. "What happened to your wings?"

"I haven't won my wings yet," Clarence admitted, a little embarrassed. "That's why I'm an angel second class."

"I don't know whether I'd like it very much, being seen around with an angel without any wings," said George, playing along.

Clarence took it as a sign that George believed him. He put his hand on George's shoulder. "I've got to earn them," he explained, "and you'll help me, won't you?"

It was obvious to George that arguing with Clarence would get him nowhere. "Sure, sure. How?" he said weakly.

Clarence smiled. "By letting me help you."

That was rich. "Only one way you can help me. You don't happen to have eight thousand bucks on you, do you?"

Clarence chuckled. "Oh, no, no. We don't use money in heaven."

"Oh, that's right. I keep forgetting. Comes in pretty handy down here, bub."

Clarence waved him off. "Oh, tut, tut . . . "

"I found it out a little late," George said. "I'm worth more dead than alive." He thought that was rather ironic.

Clarence laid his hand on George's shoulder. "Now, look, you mustn't talk like that. I won't get my wings with that attitude. You just don't know all that you've done. If it hadn't been for you—"

"Yeah, if it hadn't been for me, everybody'd be a lot better off—my wife and my kids and my friends. Look, little fella, go off and haunt somebody else, will you?"

Clarence looked worried. "No, you don't understand. I've got my job."

"Aw, shut up, will you?"

Clarence stood back and raised his eyes to heaven. "Oh, this isn't going to be so easy," he fretted. But he wasn't quitting. "So you still think killing yourself would make everyone feel happier, eh?"

"Oh, I don't know," said George, aggravated. "I guess you're right. I suppose it would have been better if I'd never been born at all."

"What did you say?" Clarence said.

"I said I wish I'd never been born!" George fired back.

"Oh, you mustn't say things like that," Clarence urged. The little man looked up thoughtfully and talked to the ceiling for a minute. "Wait a minute. Wait a minute. That's an idea. What do you think? . . . Yeah, that'll do it, all right." Clarence folded his arms and announced to George: "You've got your wish. You've never been born."

Bam! The door flew open, and the wind blasted in. Clarence hurried over to shut it. Leaning across the doorway against the wind in his nightshirt, he almost looked as if he could fly.

"You don't have to make all that fuss about it," Clarence said, looking out the open door.

"What did you say?" George asked.

"You've never been born," Clarence reminded him. "You don't exist. You haven't a care in the world."

16

George rubbed his left ear. It felt as if something was in there.

"No worries, no obligations, no eight thousand dollars to get, no Potter looking for you with the sheriff—"

"Say something else in that ear," George interrupted him.

"Sure." Clarence leaned over and said, "You can hear out of it."

He was right. "That's the doggonedest thing . . . I haven't heard anything out of that ear since I was a kid. Must have been that jump in the cold water."

"Your lip's stopped bleeding, too, George," Clarence reported.

George put his hand to his lip. "What do you know about that," he whispered. "What's happened?" He glanced out the window. "It stopped snowing out, didn't it? What's happened here?" He shook his head. It didn't matter. "What I need is a couple of good, stiff drinks," he said quickly. "How about you, angel—you want a drink? Come on, as soon as these clothes of ours are dry—"

"Our clothes *are* dry," said Clarence.

He was right again. "What do you know about that," George muttered a second time. "Stove's hotter'n I thought. Now, come on, get your clothes on, and we'll stroll up to my car and get . . ." George paused. He'd almost forgotten. Clarence was an angel, wasn't he? He probably didn't need to walk. "I'm sorry," George said. "I'll stroll, you fly." That should be interesting, he thought.

"I can't fly," Clarence pointed out. "I haven't got my wings."

He'd said that before, hadn't he? "You haven't got your wings. Yeah, that's right."

So they walked.

When they got to the spot where he'd left his car, George stopped dead. The tree was there, but where was the car?

"What's the matter?" Clarence asked.

"Well, this is where I left my car, and it isn't here." It didn't make any sense.

Clarence seemed puzzled. "You have no car."

"Well, I *had* a car, and it was right here. I guess somebody moved it."

The property owner was walking by. He wished them a good evening and turned toward the house.

George stopped him. "Oh, say—hey, where's my car?"

"I beg your pardon?" The other man frowned.

"My car, my car." George was getting impatient. "I'm the fellow that owns the car that ran into your tree."

"What tree?"

"What do you mean, what tree?" George shot back. "This tree here. I ran into it. Cut a big gash in the side of it, here." George examined the trunk for the damage.

The man came close to George and sniffed his breath. "You must mean two other trees," he joked. "You had me worried. This is one of the oldest trees in Pottersville."

"Pottersville?" What did that mean? "Why, you mean Bedford Falls!"

"I mean Pottersville," the man corrected him. He'd apparently had enough of George. "Don't you think I know where I live? What's the matter with you?" he said, and left.

"Oh, I don't know," George sighed. "Either I'm off my nut, or he is—or you are," meaning Clarence.

"It isn't me." Clarence was sure of that.

"Well, maybe I left the car up at Martini's," George figured. "Come on, Gabriel."

"Clarence," Clarence said.

"Clarence, Clarence," George muttered.

Soon they came to the bar and restaurant where George had only recently gotten punched in the face.

"That's all right. Go on in," George said. "Martini's a friend of mine." Once inside, he pointed at the bar. "There's a place to sit down."

Nick wiped the bar in front of them, waiting for an order.

"Oh, hello, Nick. Hey, where's Martini?" George said.

"You want a martini?" Nick asked.

Some joke, thought George. "No, no, Martini. Your boss. Where is he?"

Nick corrected him. "Look, I'm the boss. You want a drink or don't you?"

"Okay. All right. Double bourbon, will you—quick, huh?"

"Okay," Nick said, and turned to Clarence. "What's yours?"

"I was just thinking," Clarence said. "It's been so long since I—"

"Look, mister," Nick advised him, "I'm standing here waiting for you to make up your mind."

"That's a good man," Clarence said. "I was just thinking of a flaming rum punch. No, it's not cold enough for that. Not nearly cold enough. Wait a minute . . . wait a minute . . . I got it. Mulled wine, heavy on the cinnamon, light on the cloves. Off with you, me lad, and be lively."

Nick wasn't in the mood for jokes. "Hey, look, mister, we serve hard drinks in here for men who want to get drunk fast," he said. "And we don't need any characters around to give the joint atmosphere. Is that clear? Or do I have to slip you my left for a convincer?"

Clarence looked at George. "What's he talking about?" he said.

"Nick, Nick," George said, trying to placate him. It was true; Clarence could be a pain. "Just give him the same as mine. He's okay."

"Okay." Nick seemed satisfied for the moment.

"What's the matter with him?" George wondered. "I never saw Nick act like that before."

Clarence raised his eyebrows. "You'll see a lot of strange things from now on," he warned.

George remembered the car. And the tree—which wasn't even scratched. "Oh, yeah."

Clarence turned around on his barstool and took in the room. George felt sorry for him—Clarence seemed like a little kid sometimes. "Hey, little fella," George said, "you worry me. You got someplace to sleep?"

Nick was back with a bottle. He didn't speak as he unscrewed the top.

"No," Clarence said.

"You don't, huh? Well, you got any money?" George wondered.

"No," Clarence said again.

"No wonder you jumped in the river," George said.

"I jumped in the river to save you so I could get my wings," Clarence reminded him.

"Oh, that's right," said George.

Nick punched a total on the register, and the register bell rang.

"Uh-oh," Clarence said. "Somebody's just made it."

George put his drink down on the bar. "Made what?"

"Every time you hear a bell ring," Clarence said, "it means that some angel's just got his wings."

George lowered his voice. "Look," he said, "I think maybe you better not mention getting your wings around here."

"Why?" Clarence said simply. "Don't they believe in angels?"

Nick was listening to every word. "Ah . . . yeah," George replied, squirming, "but you know—"

"Then why should they be surprised when they see one?" said Clarence.

George tried to smooth things over for Nick. "He never grew up," George explained. "He's . . ." Then George turned to Clarence. "How old are you, anyway, Clarence?"

"Two hundred and ninety-three. Next May," Clarence said.

Nick smacked his hands on the bar. "That does it!" he barked. "Out you two pixies go, through the door or out the window."

"Look, Nick, what's wrong?" George protested.

"And that's another thing," Nick huffed. "Where do you come off calling me Nick?"

George was confused. "Well, Nick, that's your name."

"What's that got to do with it?" Nick said. "I don't know you from Adam's off ox."

Just then old man Gower appeared. He looked different from the respectable pharmacist George remembered. He seemed smaller. His hair was a mess, and he needed a shave. His eyes looked moist and worried.

Nick hollered at him. "Hey, you! Rummy, there! Come here. Come here!"

Gower shuffled toward the bar with a submissive smile on his face. He had a bleary, vacant look to his eyes.

Nick scolded him. "Didn't I tell you never to come panhandling around here, huh?" He pulled a seltzer bottle from under the bar and doused the old man's head. The customers laughed.

George was horrified. "Mr. Gower! Mr. Gower, this is George Bailey," he pleaded. "Don't you know me?"

Gower looked at him without expression. "No."

"Throw 'em out, throw 'em out!" someone in the crowd jeered.

George was frantic. "Mr. Gower . . . hey, what is this?" Why were they treating each other this way? "Hey, Nick, Nick—isn't that Mr. Gower, the druggist?"

Nick gave George the same look he might give a fly. "You know, that's another reason for me not to like you. That rumhead spent twenty years in jail for poisoning a kid. If you know him, you must be a jailbird yourself." He called another man over. "Would you show these gentlemen to the door?" he said sarcastically.

"Sure!" the big man said, and grabbed them by their jackets. "This way, gentlemen." The crowed laughed and jeered as he tossed them out.

Nick punched a total on the register and the bell sounded. "Hey! Get me!" he laughed. "I'm giving out wings!"

George and Clarence lay in a heap on the snow.

"You see, George," Clarence pointed out, "you were not there to stop Gower from putting that poison into the capsules."

"What do you mean, I wasn't there?" George exploded. "I remember distinctly . . ." Then he noticed the sign outside the bar. "What the . . . hey, what's going on around here?" he said.

The neon sign had said MARTINI'S for as long as George could remember. But not that night. Now it said NICK'S.

"Why, this ought to be Martini's place," George said. Something weird was going on, and George was getting pretty fed up with it all. He glared at his companion. This all had started when he pulled Clarence out of the river. "Look, who are you?" he demanded.

"I told you, George. I'm your guardian angel," Clarence said mildly.

"Yeah, yeah, I know. You told me that. What else are you? What? Are you a hypnotist?"

Clarence smiled. "No, of course not."

"Well, then, why am I seeing all these strange things?" George wanted to know.

"Don't you understand, George? It's because you were not born."

That didn't make any sense. "If I wasn't born, who am I?"

"You're nobody," Clarence said brightly. "You have no identity."

"What do you mean, no identity?" George huffed. "My name's George Bailey." George fumbled for his wallet.

"There is no George Bailey," Clarence said. "You have no papers, no cards, no driver's license, no four-F card . . . no insurance policy."

George jammed his fingers into the little watch pocket near his waist.

"They're not there, either," Clarence said patiently.

"What?"

"Zuzu's petals."

George began to wonder. What about Zuzu? If George didn't exist . . . no, he didn't want to think about that.

"You've been given a great gift, George," Clarence announced proudly. "A chance to see what the world would be like without you."

"No, wait a minute here. Wait a minute here." Things like this simply didn't happen. There had to be an explanation. "Aw, this is some sort of a funny dream I'm having here. So long, mister," he snapped at Clarence. "I'm going home."

"Home? What home?" Clarence said.

"Now, shut up!" George yelled. "Cut it out! You're . . . you're . . . you're crazy. That's what I think. You're screwy, and you're driving me crazy, too! I'm seeing things. I'm going home and see my wife and family. Do you understand that? And I'm going home alone."

Clarence looked up at the starry sky above. "How am I doing, Joseph?" he said. When he got his answer, he nodded. "Thanks." He started to follow after George, then turned around and looked up again, as if he'd heard a question.

"No," Clarence said. "I didn't have a drink."

17

George headed downtown, his way lighted by garish neon signs—one announcing GIRLS GIRLS GIRLS, another advertising the Bamboo Room for cocktails, and a third above a quick-cash pawnshop. Jazz music and raucous shouts filled the cold night air. Bedford Falls didn't look anything like he remembered it. Where was Gower's Drugstore? Where was the Bijou Theater?

George stopped in front of a small building that should have been the Bailey Brothers Building and Loan Association. Instead the sign read DIME A DANCE—WELCOME JITTERBUGS. "Hey . . . hey, where did the building and loan move to?" George asked a policeman who was heading for a mob scene.

"The building and what?" the cop said with a frown.

"The Bailey Building and Loan," George said plainly. "It was up there!"

The cop shook his head. "Oh, they went out of business years ago."

Suddenly George saw a familiar face at the center of a melee in front of the dime-a-dance joint. "Hey, Violet!" he yelled. She didn't hear him; she was fighting like a cat against the policemen who were hauling her toward a paddy wagon.

"Hey, listen," George said to the cop, "that's Violet Bick!"

"I know, I know." It appeared the officer knew Violet—only too well. There was a raid going on at the club, and Violet was at the center of it.

George stared at her gaudy clothes, her face paint garish in the neon light.

"That sailor's a liar!" she screamed at the policeman who held her. "I know every big shot in this town! I know Potter, and I'll have you kicked off the police force!"

"I know that girl!" George cried out.

"I know, I know, take a walk—beat it!" the cop snarled, shoving him away.

Just then George spotted Ernie's cab. He ran up to the window.

"Hey, Ernie! Ernie! Ernie, take me home. I'm off my nut!" George begged him.

Ernie regarded him coolly. "Where do you live?"

George smiled weakly. "Aw, now, doggone it, Ernie. Don't you start pulling that stuff. You know where I live. Three-twenty Sycamore. Now, hurry up." George hopped into the backseat.

"Three-twenty Sycamore?"

"Yeah, hurry up. Zuzu's sick," George barked.

"All right," Ernie agreed, and drove off.

George felt better riding in the familiar backseat of Ernie's cab. At least that hadn't changed. Maybe Ernie could help him get some answers. "Look, Ernie," George said. "Straighten me out here. I've got some bad liquor or something. Listen to me. Now, you are Ernie Bishop, and you live in Bailey Park with your wife and kid. That's right, isn't it?"

Ernie frowned suspiciously. "You seen my wife?" he asked.

"Seen your wife? I've been to your house a hundred times!" George cried.

"Look, bud, what's the idea?" Ernie came back at him. "I live in a shack in Potter's Field, my wife ran away three years ago and took the kid, and I ain't never seen you before in my life, see?"

George gave up. "Okay. Just step on it. Just get me home."

Ernie passed Bert the cop and secretly gestured for him to follow. In a few minutes both the taxi and the police car stopped in front of the vacant, ramshackle Granville place. George stared at the overgrown front yard and the broken windows. Not a single light burned in the whole house.

"Is this the place?" Ernie asked him.

"Of course it's the place!" George said bitterly.

"This house ain't been lived in for twenty years," Ernie said.

Bert walked up. "What's up, Ernie?" he said.

"I don't know, but we'd better keep an eye on this guy. He's bats," the taxicab driver told him.

George jumped out of the cab and raced through the darkened, deserted house. Where was all the furniture? What had happened to all the work Mary had done to make the old place a cozy home? It looked like a haunted house, held together by spiderwebs, the floor littered with debris.

"Mary! Mary!" he pleaded, his voice echoing through the empty rooms. "Tommy! Petey! Janie! Zuzu! Where are you?" George felt as if his heart would burst.

"They're not here, George," came a voice. "You have no children."

Clarence! He'd suddenly appeared out of nowhere. All of this was his fault. George spun around, furious, itching to get his hands on the man. "Where are they?" he roared. "What have you done with them?"

"All right, put up your hands," Bert the cop called into the house. He stood in the broken doorway, silhouetted against the light from the streetlamp. "No fast moves," he ordered. "Come on out here, both of you."

George ran to his friend. "Bert! Thank heaven you're here!" he gasped.

"Stand back," Bert warned him, raising his gun.

"Bert, what's happened to this house?" George cried. "Where's Mary? Where's my kids?"

"Watch him, Bert," Ernie said nervously, coming up behind the cop.

Bert tried reasoning with the obviously troubled man. "Come on, come on, now."

"Bert—Ernie! What's the matter with you two guys?" You were here on my wedding night. You, both of you, stood out there on the porch and sang to us, don't you remember?"

Bert and Ernie exchanged glances.

"Think I'd better be going," Ernie said, alarmed.

Bert took hold of George's arm. "Look, now, why don't you be a good kid, and we'll take you right to a doctor. Everything's going to be all right."

But George was beginning to believe that nothing was going to be all right ever again. "Bert, now, listen to me," he tried one last time, struggling to slip free of Bert's hold. "Ernie, will you take me over to my mother's house? Bert! Listen, it's that fellow here." He pointed at Clarence. "He says he's an angel. He tried to hypnotize me!"

"I hate to do this, fella," Bert said as he raised his billy club. Before he could bring it down, Clarence jumped up and bit his hand.

"Yow!" Bert cried out.

"Run, George! Run!" Clarence yelled. "Help! Joseph—help!"

Bert had Clarence on his back on the ground by this time, struggling to put handcuffs on the loony old man. "Oh, shut up!" he ordered.

"Help!" Clarence screamed, rolling on the ground. "Oh, Joseph, Joseph!"

And then he completely disappeared.

Bert knelt there a moment, groping the air where Clarence

had been—and then his mind caught up with his eyes. "Where'd he go? Where'd he go?" he cried, frantically looking around, his hands trembling. "I had him right here."

Peering around a tree, Ernie did a double take. Shaken, he waved his hand at Bert to shush him. "I need a drink."

Bert shrugged him off. "Which way'd they go? Help me find 'em!"

But Ernie was already running for his cab.

18

George ran toward his mother's house. Lights glowed brightly through the windowpanes, and George nearly wept with joy.

Home.

He dashed up the front walk and pounded up the wide wooden steps onto the porch, gasping as his hands touched the door.

Through the lace curtain covering the door's window, he could see movement, hear the sound of many voices.

He rapped on the door, jabbed the buzzer, tapped at the glass. As he waited impatiently his eyes strayed to a sign just to the left of the door, under the porch light.

MA BAILEY'S

BOARDING HOUSE

He couldn't believe his eyes. He and his brother, kidding around, had often called home the "Old Bailey Boardinghouse," but even after Peter Bailey died, his mother had never had to take in boarders.

It was a joke, George decided. That was it—Harry had arrived home from Washington and was playing some kind of joke.

George heard the door open a crack, heard his mother's voice, not soft and warm as always, but sharp and sour: "Well?"

George turned toward her. At last, someone who would take him in no matter what. Someone who could help him make sense out of all this craziness.

He caught his breath when he saw his mother's face.

She looked different—tired, haggard, the light in her eyes extinguished, her hair and clothes plain and unkempt. She peered out at George and kept a firm grip on the doorknob.

"Mother . . . ," George whispered.

Mrs. Bailey looked startled. "Mother?" she spat out. Her eyes narrowed, and so did the opening in the door. "What do you want?" she demanded sharply.

"Mother!" George cried in surprise. "This is George! I thought for sure you'd remember me. . . ."

"George who?" Mrs. Bailey responded impatiently. She shook her head and moved to close the door. "If you're looking for a room, there's no vacancy."

"Oh, Mother, please help me!" George begged desperately. "Something terrible's happened to me—I don't know what it is. Something's happened to everybody! Please let me come in, and keep me here till I get over it."

"Get over what?" Mrs. Bailey eyed his rumpled clothes, his windblown hair, his wild eyes, the stubble on his chin. Shaking her head, she said crossly, "Look, I don't take in strangers unless they're sent here by somebody I know." She started to close the door, but George blocked it with his hand.

"Well, I know everybody you know," George persisted, frantic now. How could he convince her, make his own mother remember him? "Your brother-in-law . . . Uncle Billy."

Mrs. Bailey stopped. "You know him?"

George brightened—he was getting through to her! "Well, sure I do!" he exclaimed, starting to smile.

"When'd you last see him?" she challenged.

"Today!" he said. "Over at his house."

"It's a lie!" Mrs. Bailey snapped. "He's been in the insane asylum ever since he lost his business. And if you ask me, that's where you belong, too!"

And before George could find the words to stop her, his own mother, who didn't recognize him, slammed the door in his face.

Distraught, George bolted from the porch and scrambled down the slippery walk. At the sidewalk he stopped, his breath white in the cold air as sweat poured down his face. He stared wild-eyed at the hometown that no longer claimed him and that to him seemed askew, as if in some bizarre nightmare. His mind could not grasp the meaning of it all. Paralyzed, not knowing where to go or what to do, he felt his mind reeling toward madness.

"Strange, isn't it?" Clarence said softly, leaning on Ma Bailey's mailbox. "Each man's life touches so many other lives. And when he isn't around, he leaves an awful hole, doesn't he?"

George blinked. Clarence Odbody.

George's sudden anger at this strange old man who had brought chaos to his life gave his mind something to hold on to, pulling him back from the dark abyss. George had never been a helpless sort, had always faced problems head on. He'd fight this, too.

George turned and eyed Clarence knowingly. "I've heard of things like this," he said smugly. "You've got me in some of a— a spell, or something." He began to pace, thinking hard. "Well, I'm going to get out of it. I'll get out of it! I know how, too. . . ."

George stared down the snowy street, a new look of determination on his face. "The last man I talked to before all this stuff started happening to me was Martini."

Clarence raised an eyebrow. "You know where he lives?"

"Sure I know where he lives!" George bellowed. "He lives in Bailey Park!"

Minutes later George climbed a small hill to look down on Bailey Park—or at least, what should have been Bailey Park, the neighborhood he and the Bailey Brothers Building and Loan Association had constructed from the nickels and dimes and quarters of his friends and neighbors. It should have been filled with beautiful little houses, and those houses should have been filled with ordinary families, gathered now around pianos and fireplaces and evergreen trees, celebrating Christmas Eve.

But there were no houses there. Not one.

A pale, full moon shone down on a field of tombstones that jutted up through the snow.

"Are you sure this is Bailey Park?" Clarence asked, hurrying to catch up.

George shook his head, "Ah, I'm not sure of anything anymore. All I know is this should be Bailey Park." George wandered into the cemetery, ignoring the shin-deep snow, muttering, "But where are the houses?"

"You weren't here to build them," Clarence offered.

George's gaze wandered across the headstones, scanning the simple inscriptions. Suddenly he stiffened as his eyes fell upon a modest, rounded marker. He rushed toward it, leaping over a low chain-link fence, and stumbled to his knees by the grave.

The night's ice-cold wind swept through his heart as he read the simple words etched into the stone. He ran his fingers over the deep cuts, as if he could rub away the words, make them not true.

OUR BELOVED SON

HARRY BAILEY

Clarence, standing a short distance away, declared, "Your brother, Harry Bailey, broke through the ice and was drowned at the age of nine."

Anger shot through George. He leaped to his feet, shouting like a boy defending his younger brother in a schoolyard brawl. "That's a lie!" he shouted against the wind. "Harry Bailey went to war! He got the Congressional Medal of Honor. He saved the lives of every man on that transport!"

Clarence smiled sadly and shook his head. "Every man on that transport died," he explained, as if trying to get through to a not-so-bright child. "Harry wasn't there to save them— because you weren't there to save Harry."

George turned back to the gravestone. Falling to his knees, he dug frantically with his bare hands into the snow that obscured the bottom of the marker, until at last he had revealed the final notation, numerals carved so deeply into the stone that years of snow and wind and rain could not erase them:

1911–1919

Nine years old. Harry Bailey had died when he was just nine years old.

George collapsed on the ground as all his strength left him. Grief tore his heart.

"You see, George," Clarence said softly, "you really had a wonderful life."

George gazed up at the angel, his face awash with misery.

Clarence smiled and said gently, "Don't you see what a mistake it would be to throw it away?"

"Clarence . . . ," George groaned softly.

"Yes, George?"

"Where's Mary?"

Clarence squirmed. "Well, George . . . I can't—"

George sprang up, rushed over, and grabbed the old man by the lapels of his dark overcoat. "I don't know how you know these things, but tell me—where is she?"

"I—"

"If you know where she is," George shouted desperately, tightening his grip, "tell me where my wife is!"

"I—I'm not supposed to tell—"

"Please, Clarence!" George begged. "Tell me where she is!"

"You're not going to like it, George."

"Where is she?"

"She's an old maid. She never married."

George was shaking Clarence now, nearly choking him, shouting hoarsely, "Where is she? Where is she?"

"She's just about to close up the library," Clarence blurted out.

George flung the old man to the ground and ran toward town.

Clarence Odbody, angel second class, sat up in a snowdrift and rubbed his neck. "There must be some easier way for me to get my wings. . . ."

19

George waited in front of the Pottersville Public Library as the woman in the plain hat and suit, her hair drawn back into a prim bun, backed out of the library, pulled the huge wooden door closed, and locked it. She appeared to be the last one to leave.

Maybe she'd know where Mary was.

The woman turned and walked slowly down the steps, clutching her purse close to her body, peering nervously left and right through her wire-rimmed glasses. George's eyes widened.

"Mary!"

Mary jumped back a few steps and slowly looked him over from head to toe. Then, with a small, worried frown, she hurried away in the opposite direction.

A coldness ripped through George's heart—she'd stared at him as if she'd never seen him before in her life! "Mary!"

He followed her down the street, calling her name. She glanced over her shoulder and walked faster and faster, like a woman who knows she's being followed by a strange man. She began to run. He shouted her name and ran after her, shoving people aside on the busy street, crying out for her, until finally he captured her in his arms.

"Mary! Mary, it's George. Don't you know me?" he asked. "What's happened to us?"

"I don't know you," Mary gasped. "Let me go!" She struggled against his hold, pummeling his chest with her small fists. People on the street were beginning to stop, watching with concern.

"Mary, please! Oh, don't do this to me," George begged, clutching her even closer, unable—unwilling—to accept that his Mary wouldn't somehow see through all this lunacy and know him. Mary could help him find the answers—his mother had said so, long ago. She too couldn't be lost to him. "Please, Mary, help me! Where's our kids? I need you, Mary!"

Mary Hatch's high-pitched scream filled the street as she finally broke free and ran.

Several men surrounded George and held him back, but he fought them off and struggled through the crowd. "Let me go—let me go! Mary, help me!" he shouted, following his wife as she ran screaming into the nearest nightclub.

The place was packed with people dancing and celebrating, and more people were crowding in from the street behind George. Mary shoved her way through to the bar and cowered between two women, who moved around her protectively. "That man—he's chasing me!" she shouted. "Somebody stop him!"

The music halted. Laughter turned to curious murmurs as the crowd surrounded George to prevent him from reaching Mary.

These were George's friends and neighbors, people he'd gone to school with, played ball with, grown up with—people he'd worked with through the building and loan, people he'd seen on the streets of Bedford Falls every day for years. "Tom! Ed! Charlie!" They didn't know him. Desperate, George pointed at Mary. "That's my wife!"

Mary screamed and collapsed into the women's arms.

"Mary!" George screamed, sobbing her name, fighting to get to her, but the crowd held him back.

"No, you don't!" a man shouted.

"Somebody call the police!"

"Somebody hit him on the head with a bottle!"

"We need a straitjacket!"

A siren cut through the noise of the mob, and George's head snapped up.

"Get out of here," someone snarled as the crowd shoved him toward the door.

If ever he needed a guardian angel, wingless or not—

"Clarence! Clarence!" George shrieked.

A police car pulled up and an officer jumped out just as George was shoved into the street.

"Oh, it's you!" Bert exclaimed.

Breaking free from the crowd, George threw all his strength and pain and madness into a punch that sent Bert tumbling to the ground. Stunned, the crowd allowed him to escape down the snowy street.

Bert scrambled to his feet and pulled his gun. "Stand back!" he shouted to the crowd, and fired.

The shots missed, and George fled across the square. Bert jumped into his police car and turned on the siren as he started in pursuit.

Minutes later George was back at the snowy bridge. He bolted down the pedestrian walkway and slid to a stop near the spot where this craziness had all begun—where he'd first laid eyes on his guardian angel.

"Clarence! Clarence!" he called, searching the bridge and the dark waters below for some sign of the only being left in the world who seemed to know him.

The night was dark and empty, even the gatehouse deserted,

and the dark, turbulent waters below devoured his pitiful cries.

He was alone.

It was at that moment that he believed. He believed every word the angel had told him, and he knew he was lost.

He no longer cared just for himself. He cared about his wife, his family, his friends, the town—and he couldn't bear what had become of the people he loved.

"Help me, Clarence!" he cried, clutching the railing, giving himself up to his prayers as the sharp, icy wind whistled through the bridge. "Get me back. Get me back. I don't care what happens to me, only get me back to my wife and kids. Help me, Clarence, please. Please!

"I want to live again!"

20

The police car careened around the curve and pulled onto the bridge where George stood, his face buried in his hands.

"I want to live again," he was praying more softly now, almost whispering, head bowed, eyes closed. "Please, God, let me live again."

As his words dissolved into sobs snow began to fall across his shoulders.

The police car came to a stop a few feet away. Bert climbed out. "Hey, George . . . George!" He crossed over the railing to the walkway where his friend stood. There was a look of concern on the policeman's face. "You all right? Hey, what's the matter?"

George's head came up slowly. He straightened and raised his fists, ready for a fight. "Now get out of here, Bert, or I'll hit you again! Get out of here!" he growled.

"What the Sam Hill you yelling for, George?" Bert asked, surprised.

George pulled back his arm, ready to let fly a punch. "You—" He stopped, staring at Bert in wonder. Had Bert called him by his name? George's face lit up with hope. "Bert, do you know me?" He touched his friend's chest, unsure whether to believe he was real or not.

"Know you? Huh! Are you kiddin'? I've been looking all over town, trying to find you. I saw your car piled into that tree down there, and I thought maybe you'd . . . hey, your mouth's bleeding. Are you sure you're all right?"

"Whadya—" George licked the corner of his mouth and tasted the fresh blood. He wiped at his mouth and saw red on his fingertips. The blood of life! He laughed hysterically. "My mouth's bleeding, Bert. My mouth's bleeding!"

He dug into his watch pocket. "Zuzu's petals. Zuzu—" He held the petals up in front of Bert's nose. "There they are, Bert!" he shrieked. "What do you know about that?" He flung himself at his friend, hugging him hard, then jabbed his arms straight up into the air and hollered, "Merry Christmas!"—and dashed off toward home.

Bert stared after him, nonplused, then waved. "Well, Merry Christmas!"

"Mary!" George shouted, running through the snow toward home. When he passed by his old car, crumpled against the tree, he raised his arms over his head and shouted, "Yay!" then patted it like a dog.

He ran past the town sign. It now read:

YOU ARE NOW IN BEDFORD FALLS

"Yay!" he screamed again. "Hello, Bedford Falls!" And then he was running, slipping and sliding, dashing down the streets, shouting "Merry Christmas!" to everyone he saw.

"Merry Christmas, George!" people called back cheerfully.

At the Bijou Theater, which was showing *The Bells of St. Mary's,* he shouted, "Merry Christmas, movie house!" A few more steps, and it was "Merry Christmas, Emporium!" and then "Merry Christmas, you wonderful old building and loan!" He saw lights in the bank offices across the street, ran over, and banged on the window. "Merry Christmas, Mr. Potter!"

Startled, Potter growled, "Happy New Year to you—in jail!" Reaching for the phone, he added, "Go on home—they're waiting for you."

Then finally, finally, he was home, and he nearly broke the door down, crying, "Mary! Mary!"

But instead of Mary, he found several very stern-looking men, including a newspaper photographer, a deputy, and Mr. Carter.

"Well, hello, Mr. Bank Examiner!" George exclaimed, shaking the man's hand with enthusiasm and affection.

"Mr. Bailey," Carter barked. "There's a deficit."

"I know," George cried. "Eight thousand dollars!"

"George," said the town deputy, "I've got a little paper here—"

"I'll bet it's a warrant for my arrest," George interrupted. "Isn't it wonderful? I'm going to jail. Merry Christmas!"

Flash! The photographer got that on film.

"Reporters?" George exclaimed gleefully, then he dashed into the living room, looking around. "Where's Mary? Mary! Oh, look at this wonderful old drafty house," he exclaimed as he crossed the hall. "Mary! Mary!" He staggered back to the stunned gentlemen. "Have you seen my wife?"

"Merry Christmas, Daddy!"

George looked up to the stair landing and thought he'd burst with joy when he spotted three of his darling children, dressed in their pajamas, smiling down at him. "Kids!"

He ran up the stairs and—

"Uh-oh." The newel post knob came off in his hands, as always, only this time he kissed it before jiggling it lovingly back into place. "Kids! Pete! Janie! Tommy!" He fell to his knees and gathered them into his arms as the photographer downstairs took another shot. "Oh, I could eat you up! Where's your mother?"

"She went looking for you," Janie said, "with Uncle Billy."

"Daddy!" Zuzu burst from her room and threw her arms around his neck.

"Zuzu—Zuzu! My little gingersnap. How do you feel?"

"Fine."

Janie nodded. "And not a smidge of temperature!"

"And not a smidge—" George laughed uproariously. "Hallelujah!"

At that moment Mary flung open the door and came inside, surprised to find the four gentlemen in her front hall. "Hello." And then she saw her husband upstairs with the children.

"George! Darling!"

"Mary! Mary!" He turned to come downstairs, and Zuzu jumped up on his back.

Mary pounded up the stairs. "George, darling! Where have you been?"

They met midway, hugging, kissing, surrounded by laughing children.

George took her face in his hands. "Oh, let me touch you, let me touch you. Are you real?"

Mary was breathless, laughing, excited, trying to tell him something. "George—"

"You have no idea what's happened to me," George told her.

"*You* have no idea what's happened," she replied, her voice intense with joy. "Well, come on, George, come on downstairs, quick. They're on their way." She grabbed his hand.

"All right." He was giddy now, with Zuzu on his back, Tommy under one arm, and Janie and Pete following closely on his heels.

"Come on in here," Mary said, leading him into the living room. "Now, you stand right over here, by the tree. Right there, and don't move. Don't move!" She swept the papers off the table where Pete had been writing earlier that night, then turned toward the door, her eyes shining, her voice brimming with laughter. "I hear them coming now. George, it's a miracle. It's a miracle!"

George was barely listening; all he wanted to do was kiss her, and hold her and the kids, and never let go. But Mary wriggled from his arms and ran to the front door.

"What's happening?" Zuzu cried.

"Who's coming, Daddy?" asked Pete.

"Come in, Uncle Billy!" Mary cried. "Everybody! In here!"

Billy tottered in, carrying a wide wicker laundry basket by the handles, leading a parade of snow-covered neighbors into the living room.

"George!" he cried. "George! Here's everything right here." He dumped the contents of the basket onto the table.

Money. Crumpled dollar bills, quarters, dimes. A whole bushel basket full of money.

"Isn't it wonderful?" Billy burst out. "Mary did it, George! Mary did it! She told a few people you were in trouble, and they scattered all over town collecting money. They didn't ask any questions, just said, 'If George is in trouble, count on me.' You never saw anything like it. It spread like wildfire!"

George was dumbfounded. People were swarming in, friends and neighbors and customers—all the little people of Bedford Falls were turning out their pockets and pouring out their hearts.

"What is this, George, another run on the bank?" his friend Leon joked, adding his cash to the pile.

"Here you are, George. Merry Christmas!"

"Now, don't crowd, don't push," Ernie the cabdriver hollered. "The line forms on the right!"

"Merry Christmas, George, and God bless you!"

Billy stepped aside, and he and George's mother hugged each other joyfully.

George could only stand there, holding Zuzu in his arms, grinning like a fool. And what a fool he'd been.

"Hey, Mr. Martini!" Ernie called out as the man pushed through the crowd. "Merry Christmas! Step right up here."

Martini poured a huge pasta bowl full of money onto the table. "I busted the jukebox, too!" he crowed, and everybody laughed.

"Oh, Mr. Gower!" Ernie shouted, helping him through the crowd.

The pharmacist held up a glass cracker jar stuffed with bills. "I made the rounds of my charge accounts!"

Violet hurried up to the table, still dressed in furs and wearing that silly hat. "I'm not going to go, George," she said, returning his money with a grin. "I changed my mind."

"Oh, Annie, Annie!" The aging Bailey housekeeper bustled to the counter, snapping open her pocketbook.

"I've been saving this money for a divorce—if I ever get a husband!" she cackled. "Merry Christmas!"

Mr. Partridge, the school principal, sprinkled dollars onto the pile. "There you are, George. I got the faculty all up out of bed." He handed Zuzu his pocket watch. "And here's something for you to play with, baby."

Another man pushed his way to the table, calling out, "I wouldn't have a roof over my head if it wasn't for you, George."

It seemed to George as though half the town was in his living room that night, and it felt wonderful. Ernie suddenly hollered out, "Just a minute, just a minute. Quiet, everybody. Quiet—quiet! Now, get this. It's from London."

"Oh!" someone exclaimed into the room, which had suddenly fallen silent.

Ernie held up a telegram and read: "'Mr. Gower cabled you

need cash. Stop. My office instructed to advance you up to twenty-five thousand dollars. Stop. Hee-haw and Merry Christmas. Sam Wainwright.'"

The room echoed with astonished gasps, and then suddenly you couldn't hear a thing for all the cheers and excited chatter.

Standing on a chair next to the wall so she could see above the throng, Mary choked back her tears and sought George's eyes across the crowd.

George gazed into her face and felt overwhelmed by the wonder of it all. He buried his face in Zuzu's shoulder, unable to count his blessings because they were far, far too numerous.

"Mr. Martini, how about some wine?" Mary's suggestion was greeted with cheers. The glasses were passed around.

Janie asked her mother if now was a good time to play her song, and Mary said yes. The little girl dashed to the piano in her pajamas and robe and began her earnest chords of "Hark the Herald Angels Sing"—and as the Baileys' family and friends and neighbors joined in, filling the drafty old house with rich, joyful harmony, George thought it was the most beautiful carol he'd ever heard.

The mood was so infectious that even Mr. Carter, the bank examiner, made his way to the miracle table. Reluctantly he dug some bills from his pocket, frowned at them as if he thought this whole escapade was the most ridiculous thing he'd ever seen, and then dropped the money onto the pile. His voice was surprisingly loud and joyous as he moved away and joined in the singing.

Just behind him, the doom-faced deputy shoved his way to the table, dark mustache twitching. He too dug into his pocket, but instead of cash, he withdrew the warrant for George's arrest. He held it out toward George and Mary, then, laughing, ripped it in half and tossed it on the pile.

Through it all, Eustace sat at the table, joyfully totaling the money on his adding machine.

Suddenly a shout went up—"Harry Bailey!"

George looked up in astonishment. His brother wasn't due in until the next day! But there he was, the handsome young hero, his dark uniform speckled with snow, grabbing his older brother's hand and flashing him that dashing smile of his. "George, you old son of a gun!"

"Harry," George exclaimed, his voice breaking. "Harry!" Mere hours ago he had knelt at his brother's grave, and now here he was, strong and tall and alive.

"Looks like I got here too late," Harry said to Mary, glancing at the huge pile of money.

Bert the cop was right behind him, with his old accordion strapped across his uniform. "Mary, I got him here from the airport just as quick as I could. The fool flew all the way up here in a blizzard."

"Harry, how about your banquet in New York?" Mrs. Bailey asked.

"Oh, I left right in the middle of it, as soon as I got Mary's telegram."

Ernie passed him a glass of wine.

"Good idea, Ernie," Harry acknowledged. "A toast . . ." The room quieted. "To my big brother, George—the richest man in town!"

George choked up, looking around at his family and friends. And in a heartbeat, he knew his brother Harry was right.

Bert began to play his accordion, leading them all into a different song: "Should auld acquaintance be forgot and never brought to mind . . ."

Tears of joy welled up in George's eyes, and as he glanced down to brush them away, he noticed a small white book lying on top of the pile of money. Astonished, he picked it up and read the title: *The Adventures of Tom Sawyer,* by Mark Twain.

Little Zuzu helped him open the cover. There, opposite the title page, was an inscription in rather old-fashioned handwriting.

Dear George:

Remember, no man is a failure
who has friends.
Thanks for the wings!

Love,
Clarence

Mary read over George's shoulder and asked, "What's that?"

George grinned. "It's a Christmas present from a very dear friend of mine."

Behind them, a tiny bell rang. Zuzu pointed over her father's shoulder at a small bell hanging from a branch of the Christmas tree. "Look, Daddy. Teacher says every time a bell rings, an angel gets his wings."

"That's right," George said. "That's right!" He hugged his wife and daughter tight, glanced heavenward, and winked.

"Atta boy, Clarence!"